A Literary Confection

*A collection of 26 stories and poems
by prize-winning & published writers*

by LiterEight
a group of eight Scottish-based female writers

Published in Kindle by LiterEight.2012
This paperback edition published by LiterEight 2013
Copyright © LiterEight 2012

All rights reserved.
No part of this book may be reproduced, stored in a retrieval system, or transmitted in any form or by any means (electronic, mechanical, photocopy, sound or digital recording) or translated into any language, without prior written permission from members of LiterEight, except by a reviewer who may quote brief passages in a review.

The rights of the authors have been asserted by them in accordance with section 77 of the Copyright, Designs and Patents Act 1988. Individually they are free to re-publish elsewhere their copyright works that appear in this book.

www.litereight.co.uk

ISBN 978-1482745467

ACKNOWLEDGEMENTS

The authors would like to thank award-winning playwright and novelist, Catherine Czerkawska, and author and playwright Cally Phillips for their support in the creation of this anthology, web designer John Atchison for all his technical support, and illustrator Maggie Bolton for designing the cover artwork.

A Literary Confection

Dip into our literary confection and taste the delicious and tempting variety inside. You'll find colourful and flavoursome stories and poems, some soft-centred, others perhaps a little darker with a hint of bitterness, a bit of humbug and the occasional crunchy nut.

The Untimely End of Elvira Carrington   short story by Maggie Bolton…..7

Cards at the Ready   mini story by Fiona Atchison…..13

Web of Intrigue   short story by Helena Sheridan…..15

Rough Ride   poem by Greta Yorke…..20

Honeysuckle Cottage   short story by Janice Johnston….21

Birthday Girl   mini story by Lesley Deschner…..30

Framed   short story by Helena Sheridan …..31

Nightfall   mini story by Catherine Lang…..36

Clearances   poem by Greta Yorke …..38

Imitation of Life   poem by Lesley Deschner…..39

Tongue-Tied   short story by Fiona Atchison …..40

Autumn Shades   poem by Fiona McFadzean…..49

Photographic Memory   short story by Catherine Lang…50

Ode to an Ageing Hippie   poem by Helena Sheridan….57

True Love   short story by Janice Johnston …..58

Batch Baker   mini story by Fiona Atchison …..63

Pageant Day   short story by Fiona McFadzean…..64

Final Move   poem by Fiona Atchison…..70

Sauce for the Goose short story by Catherine Lang…..72

Honeymoon in Rome poem by Maggie Bolton…..79

Teacher's Pet short story by Janice Johnston…..81

The Rock poem by Fiona McFadzean…..87

Getting Plastered poem by Catherine Lang…..88

Cutting Loose short story by Helena Sheridan…..90

The Full Works mini story by Greta Yorke….. 94

A Bit of Peace & Quiet short story by Maggie Bolton …95

The LiterEight Writers…..103

The Untimely End of Elvira Carrington
by Maggie Bolton

She was sitting at the computer in her study; a natural place, surely, for a novelist to be. What was definitely not natural, however, was the way she was sprawled inelegantly over the arm of the swivel chair, one hand dangling. Her mouth was open and her face empty.

"Aunt Elvira?" I said.

I touched her arm and something dropped onto the carpet with a dull thud. It was a small, silver pistol. There was a neat, dark hole in her temple beneath the immaculately styled hair. Elvira Carrington was quite, quite dead.

On the TV or in one of Aunt Elvira's books, they always scream when they find a body, don't they? I didn't scream. I admit I didn't feel too good and my heart was thumping wildly, but I didn't scream. I didn't actually do anything for a while. I just stood there, shaking. No doubt it was shock.

I must have called the police and done other practical things, but I really don't remember. Normally, I suppose, people call the rest of the family. That wasn't necessary in this case as there's only me. People came. A doctor pronounced her dead, though you'd hardly need a degree in medicine to work that out. They took her away very quietly and discreetly, then sat me down and made me a cup of tea. I remember thinking it should have been me doing that – it usually is. All I could think was that things would never be the same again and, frankly, I wasn't sorry about that. That sounds heartless when they'd just carted away my aunt in a body bag, but the truth is that Elvira Carrington was not a very nice woman.

Detective Inspector McKay was the man in charge. He had a lovely accent, just like Sean Connery. But his eyes were very direct and sharp, as if they could probe deep into your soul and winkle out any little secrets that might be hidden there. I avoided looking at him. I looked at my hands mostly, scrunching up a damp paper hanky and pulling it to bits.

He wanted to know how I found her; if I'd touched anything; if I'd heard the shot; if there was anyone else in the house – that sort of thing. I answered as best I could. I told him no, there was no one else in the house and that when I touched her arm the gun fell.

"So it was definitely in her hand?" he asked.

"Of course it was," I said. "Well, it must have been, mustn't it? She…" I could hardly bring myself to say it. "She shot herself, didn't she?"

"Hmm," he said, tapping his teeth with his finger-nail as he considered the matter, "…and you say you heard the shot?"

"Yes," I said, "well, I heard something, but I was in the kitchen you see, on the phone. That's right at the other end of the house."

"You were on the phone?" he said, looking interested.

"Yes. I was ringing Alex Dunbar – that's her agent. She wasn't really herself this morning and I was a bit concerned about her. He said not to worry and he'd be coming up to see her tomorrow anyway, as he'd heard some rather disturbing rumours. Then there was this noise. Alex said 'What was that?' or something and I said it sounded like a car backfiring. It was a few minutes later when I found her that I realised it must have been..."

"So he heard the shot too. Check on that, Atkins," he said to some youth in a trench coat who was trying to look important. Then he turned to me again. "Have you told Mr Dunbar what's happened?"

"Oh dear," I said. "No, I didn't think. I should ring and tell him. He'd have a wasted journey tomorrow."

"I think Detective Constable Atkins can attend to that, Miss Carrington."

He did that annoying tapping thing again and then went over what I'd already told him. By his frown I took it that he was not entirely satisfied.

"Can you think of any reason why your aunt would want to take her own life? She was a very successful woman. Surely she had everything to live for?"

I looked down at my hands again and shook my head. It would ruin her reputation, but she was dead, so what did it matter now?

"It was all going to come out you see," I said. "I suppose she couldn't face it."

My paper hanky was totally in shreds by now, but I still clutched it.

"Her books, the ones that were such a success," I went on, "...well, she didn't write them. It was Uncle Henry. She just found his manuscripts in a drawer after she... I mean, after he died. She brought them up to date, passed them off as her own, and bingo – overnight success. But then the publishers wanted more of the same and she couldn't do it. Her last book was terrible; the critics panned it. She was trying to write another one but that wasn't working either. Then this morning...well, it seems someone found out."

I looked at McKay to see how he was taking all this. He nodded as if it made sense.

"I feel terribly disloyal telling you this," I said, "I know she was...difficult at times, but she was my only relative. She and Uncle Henry took me in you know when I had a nerv...when I was ill, after my parents died. I was only fifteen. I've lived here ever since. Then it was poor Uncle Henry and now Aunt Elvira. I have no one left in the world."

Detective Inspector McKay patted me awkwardly on the shoulder. But the moment was spoiled by that youth coming back, all cock-a-hoop, to say that Mr Dunbar confirmed the time and details of the phone-call.

"So, time of death two-thirty then," he said eagerly.

They left soon after that. I assured them I would be perfectly fine alone. They were very kind. There would be an inquest of course, but Detective Inspector McKay was sure the verdict would be suicide.

The house – *My* house – seemed very big and empty after they'd gone. I thought the situation called for a stiff brandy – it had, after all, been an eventful day. Sipping quietly, I frowned as I recalled my last conversation with my aunt. The nerve of the woman!

"I've decided to sell the house," she said – just like that, as if I had no say in the matter. "I shall go and live in Spain. I'm giving up writing. I'm just completely burned out. I suppose you could come if you like, but perhaps you'd rather take some of the cash and er...well, do whatever you want really. You're a big girl now. It's time you learned to stand on your own two feet."

She turned away but I knew she was sneering.

"But you can't," I said. "This is my home for as long as I want. It said so in Uncle's will."

She just shrugged. "Sorry, but I shall need the cash. The proceeds of the sale and my royalties should keep me going for a while but then..."

"Huh!" I said, "*then*, no doubt, you'll find some other sick, gullible, old man to fleece, just like you did with Uncle Henry. You married him for his money and then you poisoned him. Everybody knows that."

"*What?*" she said, "Don't be ridiculous! It wasn't poi...and anyway, what money? He left me nothing but debts, a crumbling ruin... oh, and *you!*"

"...and his manuscripts," I said.

She raised an eyebrow.

"Oh, so you know about that do you?" she said, "OK, so I used his work – so what? He owed me."

She sat there swivelling her chair, ignoring me. I could feel anger building up inside.

"You can't sell this house," I shouted. "You *can't!*"

Aunt Elvira's hand slid into her desk drawer.

"Calm down, dear," she said, "don't excite yourself. You know what happens when you get overwrought. I'll get your tablets and we'll talk about it another time when you're more rational."

I saw the glint of silver in her hand and I knew what it was. She was talking about *me* being overwrought and irrational, but I wasn't the one with a gun in my hand. The anger was becoming uncontrollable. I suppose I must have had another of my 'red mist moments'. I moved at a speed which surprised me as well as Aunt Elvira. I grabbed her hand and held it to her head and then…

I took another soothing sip of brandy as I relived the scene. But you know I'm still not exactly sure which of us pulled the trigger. It was probably me. I thought the phone-call to Alex Dunbar was a nice touch. The noise he heard wasn't the gun-shot of course. It was one of those clapper toys made of two joined pieces of wood. It was always a favourite of mine. You could creep up behind people and make them jump. Such fun!

Cards at the Ready
by Fiona Atchison

A grim tension hung over the table. Four poker-faced players held their cards close. Anna glanced longingly at the firmly shut door and wished she were on the other side. Allan, however, would never forgive her if she didn't perch loyally at his shoulder.

She knew the outcome of this final game could have severe consequences if Allan scooped the pot. David Doyle wanted to win desperately and he was a notoriously bad loser. Suzie, standing behind David, looked as anxious as Anna felt. His eruptions of violence were not uncommon. Soon, the other two players were out leagued and headed off with relief.

Allan reached for his drink, took a large slug, then misjudged replacing the glass. Red liquid streamed towards the stack of banknotes. Like blood, Anna thought as she searched her bag for tissues to stop the deluge. But the players hardly noticed, so intent their concentration on the cards which would spell win or lose.

Seconds later, the final card slapped down. Anna and Suzie exchanged worried glances. David had lost. There was a long silence until:

"You won, good game." David spoke through gritted teeth.

Allan slowly pulled his winnings towards him, "Thanks."

Suzie exhaled. "That was close," she whispered to Anna, "I thought I was going to have to hold David back."

"I know," smiled Anna, as she mopped blackcurrant juice from the Monopoly money. "It's amazing how five-year-olds become so competitive playing Snap. Now, I wonder where our cowardly husbands have sloped off to?"

Web of Intrigue
by Helena Sheridan

Daniel Corin braced himself as the bus splashed through another rain-filled pot hole.

"You're crazy!" His agent's harsh words echoed in his mind. Admittedly, with the deadline of his next novel looming ever closer, his sudden decision to go back to Ireland did seem irresponsible but there was nothing else he could do. The arrival of the mysterious e-mail had changed everything.

"Forever Yours, E."

The familiar greeting had sent an icy shiver coursing through his body. Wild excitement quickly replaced logic. Perhaps he had been foolish to agree to the bizarre meeting but the series of personal communications had finally convinced him...somehow Erin was alive!

Daniel's expression hardened as he remembered the horrible crash that had reportedly claimed the life of his first love. Heart-wrenching memories of the burned out coach continued to haunt him. "No survivors." He could still hear the broadcaster's cold delivery of the agonising news.

The passing years had not lessened the pain of losing Erin. Instead he had been plagued by a catalogue of unanswered questions. Why had she taken that early bus without telling him and where had she been going?

With a deep sigh, he drew a gloved hand over the misty window and peered out at the rugged coastline. How he hoped that joy would soon replace his lonely years of anguish.

Dipping into his jacket pocket he extracted the faded photo that had long become his most treasured possession. An attractive couple in colourful gear smiled back at him from the dog-eared print. Erin's youthful image still warmed his heart.

With a wry smile he considered their hippy fashions and unruly hair-dos. Yes, there had been many changes since those carefree days, he thought, sweeping his hand over his now balding head, but Erin had always remained special.

The portly conductor zig-zagged his way to the front of the bus.

"Sure you want off here, sir?" he answered Daniel's signal to stop. "It's a bit isolated."

Daniel gave a determined nod. Then, raising his collar against the shrewd appraisal of his fellow passengers, he clambered from the bus.

By morning his 'return' would be local gossip, he considered, just as his boisterous antics had prompted criticism all those years ago. Unfairly labelled the 'wild lad' of the district, it was little wonder Erin's parents had opposed their relationship.

His eyes sparkled as he recalled their 'secret rendezvous'. Nothing had kept them apart then and nothing would separate them now.

Determined to adhere to Erin's instructions that they meet 'at their special place', he hastened down the overgrown path that led to the sandy cove.

The specific details helped dispel any lingering doubts. Only Erin knew of the windswept inlet where they had spent so much time together. The jagged rocks that skirted the coastline had proved the perfect cover for their covert meetings. There they had laughed and loved, safe from the prying eyes and condemnation of the gossipy villagers above.

"I'll be waiting for you tomorrow, as always... E."

Daniel had been quick to spot the vital clue in her final message.

They had 'always' met, at sunset in the tiny cove. Now she would return to him appropriately, perhaps, on the anniversary of her 'death'.

A sombre mist crept in from the sea, brushing his pale cheeks with a chilling caress. Glancing anxiously about the deserted cove, Daniel felt his heart sinking with every passing minute.

His frantic pacing left a clutter of footprints on the damp shore as he fought to repel the negative thoughts somersaulting in his mind.

What if Erin had not sent the e-mail, then who? Success had brought a barrage of fans and well-wishers, all eager to learn more about the author, and express their views, complimentary or otherwise, on his latest literary work. Perhaps the strange messages were nothing more than a cruel joke from a jealous rival, who had learned of his past love. His stomach lurched at the sickening prospect.

Fame certainly had its drawbacks. He loathed the giddy whirl of endless parties and social climbing friends.

Nothing, it seemed, could appease his loneliness. Reluctantly he recalled the ambitious brunette who had lured him to a hasty marriage. How quickly she had requested a divorce when a more lucrative offer presented itself.

Daniel sighed. Erin had been so different. She had believed in his first faltering attempts to be a writer. Had it not been for her encouragement he would have surrendered to the opinion of the rejection slips and abandoned his dream. If only he could find happiness once more.

"Erin!" he shouted, his stifled emotions exploding. "Where are you?"

The wind replied with a haunting howl. Daniel gasped as the shadowy image of a young woman appeared through the eerie gloom.

It was as if time had stilled. The ghostly mist veiled her ageless beauty. He wanted to rush forward and hold her again but felt rooted by an overwhelming blend of fear and excitement.

Warm tears trickled freely down his ashen face. Captivated, he blessed each delicate step that brought her closer. Slowly, she raised her bowed head to reveal the bitter truth.

"You're not Erin!" Daniel snarled at the impostor.

The likeness was uncanny. The same tangle of copper hair, same playful glimmer in her hazel eyes. His spirit sank at the cruel deception. Reeling with disappointment he grabbed the stranger by the arm.

"What kind of…malicious…"

The woman wrenched herself free from his firm grasp. "I'm sorry but there was no other way," she spluttered. "I had to be sure you'd come. I have to speak to you about the book."

"A reporter!" Daniel threw up his arms in disgust. "A damned reporter. I might have known. Well, if you think I'd give you an interview after you conned me…"

Fumbling in the pocket of her long coat she offered him a small diary. "I...came by this last month. It explains everything."

Daniel took hold of the slim volume. His eyes widened in recognition of the scribbled notes inside. There was no mistaking Erin's ornate scrawl. He revelled in the faint whiff of her favourite perfume lingering on the curled pages.

"It says Erin wasn't in the crash," he read, faltering over the vital passage, "she felt sick so she slipped off the bus before it happened. But I don't understand. Why did she go? Why didn't she come back?"

"She didn't want to ruin your future. You see, she was carrying your child." She paused, "My name is Evelyn. Her last wish was that I find my father."

Her nervous smile made Daniel erupt into a fresh wash of tears. Drawing Evelyn into his arms he offered a silent prayer of thanks to Erin, for at long last he had a chance of happiness again.

Rough Ride
by Greta Yorke

White horses my Gran called them,
spray crested waves spewing into frothy foam
across the firth.
Frolicking steeds metamorphose
to wild surfing stallions,
charging Camargue and Lipizzaner demons
whose power thrashes against our bow.
The vessel lunges after each crescendo
borne on equine fury.
Stampeding mustangs
resistant of break
carry us home in rampant rage.
When calmed
by some elusive whisperer,
they retire
to their stables of the deep,
tethered,
but ready for off
at the crack
of Aeolian whip.

Honeysuckle Cottage
by Janice Johnston

"Honeysuckle Cottage?" Gayle glanced up from her computer, "I don't think we're 'Honeysuckle Cottage' sort of people." Her eyes flicked back to the screen again.

Michael slumped down on the nearest chair. "Well, it was there or a park bench come Saturday night." He sighed and closed his eyes, "And if it hadn't been for Rob's aunt eloping with the postman..."

Gayle's concentration was gone. "She didn't!"

"She did. Ran off to Gretna Green last week. At this very moment they're honeymooning in Australia." He opened one eye and grinned at Gayle's expression. "Mind you, it wasn't quite the scandal it sounds. They had a big party in the village hall before they left."

"But what's Rob's aunt eloping got to do with our problem?"

"Well, her house is empty for the next few months – they're visiting relatives over there – and since we are about to be chucked out of here," he waved his arm vaguely round the impersonal flat, "Rob suggested we rent her house until we can find something more suitable."

He closed his eyes again. "The only slight problem is that it's an extra twenty minutes on the train every morning."

"Couldn't you have found something more central?" Gayle said.

"Couldn't you have realised sooner that our lease was about to run out?" he retorted. "At least I've done something."

"You know I have to get this presentation sorted out." Gayle twisted back to the screen again. "It's due next month and I've still loads to do."

"I've work I should be dealing with too, but I thought finding somewhere to stay by the weekend was kind of important – or don't you care?" It had occurred to him that maybe Gayle might use this as an excuse to move back in with her parents. It wasn't that they weren't getting on, it was more a feeling that their relationship was just bobbing along on the surface. He held his breath as he waited for her reply.

Gayle kept her back stiff as she saved the file she had been working on. She deliberately ignored his question and asked one of her own. "How soon can we move in?"

"It's frightening to think how few boxes it takes to store our life." Michael sealed the final box and glanced around. The flat should have looked bare and forlorn after he had packed away all their belongings but somehow it just looked the same. Obviously, they hadn't put down any roots in the flat, only covered the surface with clothes and CDs. The furnishings and fittings had been chosen by the rental company to look neutral. It had remained neutral for the last six months.

He turned to the only corner of the room with any personality stamped on it. "You'll have to switch off that laptop now," he said. "We need to set off with the van."

"Hang on," Gayle typed furiously, "just let me finish this section."

Michael began gathering up the paper files scattered over the floor.

"Don't mix them up!" she glanced away from the screen for a second.

"Fine." He thumped them back on the ground. It seemed as if he couldn't do anything right these days. "But if they're not in the van in the next fifteen minutes you can take them and your laptop on the train." He grabbed the last few boxes and headed down to the street.

Gayle gritted her teeth. "Don't you know this is the worst possible time for a move?" she hissed to his retreating back.

"Michael," Gayle stared through the windscreen, "this is country – I don't do country."

"Don't be ridiculous." Michael manoeuvred the van as close as possible to the garden gate. "OK, it's not city centre, but it is definitely suburbs."

"Michael, that green patch, that's a field."

"Erm," Michael fiddled with the door handle, "actually, that green patch is our garden."

Gayle stared at the expanse of lawn stretching round the cottage. "Only you could go from dying pot plant to huge garden in one easy step." She shook her head. "Not only do I not do country, I definitely don't do gardens. I'm not ready to be responsible for living things. The garden is your problem." Despite all her denials of responsibility, she paused. "What if you kill it all off before Rob's aunt gets back?"

"Don't worry," Michael shrugged, "I'll learn." But he began to look more closely at what he'd taken on. Rob's aunt had only been gone a few weeks but already he could see a smattering of weeds taking over the borders. "What's that?" Michael pointed with his toe, balancing the box he'd hauled from the back of the van precariously in his arms.

Gayle pulled out her box of files and looked round. "What?"

"That." Michael shook his foot again and the box jiggled dangerously.

"You mean those little green bits?" Gayle bent down and studied the sturdy green swords pushing up through the soil. "They're daffodils, look!" She pointed to a sheltered spot under the hedge where a yellow bud was about to open. "I've never noticed them growing," she smiled, "I usually only see them in bunches on garage forecourts." Her eyes sparkled at the thought of watching them bud then bloom, but the moment didn't last. "You'd better get another flat sorted out as soon as possible. Remember, this is only temporary." She marched up the path, ignoring other green mysteries and barely glancing at the chocolate-box cottage that was to be their new home for the time being.

On Saturday, Gayle took her toast and tea out on the decking and settled down to watch Michael. He was clutching a gardening book in one hand and a spade in the other.

"Where did you find that?" she called.

"It was on the bookshelves in the living room," Michael beamed. "It's really useful."

"Not the book, you idiot!" Gayle laughed.

"Oh, this?" Michael waved the spade, almost decapitating the latest flowers to appear. "We have a Garden Shed!" he dropped the spade as he tried to turn a page. "Why don't you come and help me?"

"I see myself in a more supervisory role," Gayle sipped her tea, "and anyway, I don't think 'earth' would match this nail varnish."

"Come on, Gayle," Michael looked disappointed, "you decipher the instructions and I'll do the work."

"I suppose…" Gayle hesitated for a second – Michael held his breath – then she shook her head. "No, I'm sorry, I still have so much work to do for the presentation."

"No, no, no!" Gayle furiously deleted page after page on the screen.

"Problems?" Michael popped his head round the wide-open French doors.

Gayle sighed loudly, "If I organise things to suit one department, the other sections are going to be totally against my proposals." She dragged her hands through her hair. "I have to find a way to please everyone, and it's not possible."

"Sounds as if you need a break. Come on," he gestured her to come outside, "some fresh air will do you good."

"Fresh air, huh, that's all I've got at the moment." But she followed him out to the garden.

Michael knelt down by a border and started to pull up weeds again. Gayle slouched beside him and began, almost absentmindedly, to weed too. "I'm never going to get everyone to agree. It's impossible.

I'll have to resign." She grabbed handfuls of weeds and threw them into the wheelbarrow.

Michael said nothing.

Gayle weeded on, mumbling to herself. Then she stopped suddenly. "I've got it!" she cried, and ran back to her computer.

Michael looked over at the large patch of now weed-free ground where she'd been working, and smiled.

Gayle paused at the door, "But I still don't do country. Remember to check out flats in the city centre. We can't keep getting up at the crack of dawn and trailing home at all hours."

His smile evaporated at her words. "It's only twenty minutes more than before," he snapped. He had been looking. All the flats he'd seen so far had been freshly decorated, spacious enough and close to the centre but he couldn't see Gayle and himself living in any of them. Not after Honeysuckle Cottage, anyway. If only Gayle could see it that way, too.

"Well, how did your presentation go?" Michael moved his briefcase to let Gayle flop down on the seat he'd been saving.

"Great!" Gayle let out a sigh. "And best of all, it's over. I can relax now. Someone else can deal with the logistics." The extra twenty minutes on the train was turning into a winding down and chatting time, something they hadn't really had time for in their hectic lives before moving to Honeysuckle Cottage.

Then there was the walk from the station.

"Look, those trees are turning into pink puffballs."

"Cherry blossom," Michael smiled. "I borrowed a book from the library. In fact," he looked at Gayle out of the corner of his eye, "I've been reading a lot about gardens."

Gayle laughed and pulled something from her briefcase, *The Idiot's Guide to Gardening*. I thought I'd better find out a bit about this gardening malarkey myself since it looks like we'll be stuck in Honeysuckle Cottage for a while yet. You don't seem to be having much luck with the hunt for a city flat."

"Ah, well," Michael looked suitably serious, "it's a difficult time of year to find a flat. The market's static – so the estate agent tells me. And we want to make sure it's absolutely right for us."

"Really?" Gayle raised an eyebrow. "That sounds like total waffle to me. Anyone would think you don't want to leave Honeysuckle Cottage."

"And you still do?" Michael raised his eyebrow even higher.

"Well..." Gayle hesitated, "it is starting to grow on me, but I'm still not sure if I'm ready for all that commitment." She shrugged, "Let's just take it a day at a time."

Looking after the garden had started out as an obligation to Rob's aunt, but now it seemed to be the heady scent of honeysuckle that drew both of them outdoors at every opportunity. Gradually their lazy weekends changed.

"My back's killing me!" Michael groaned.

"Come on, you wimp. If we get this border dug over we can buy some new plants tomorrow." She turned over another spadeful of earth.

"Then you'll make me spend all afternoon putting them in." Michael groaned again. "Don't you have a report to write, or a file to rearrange?"

"I thought you wanted me to be involved?" Gayle brushed her hair back from her eyes, inadvertently smearing soil over her cheek. "Anyway, I'm enjoying this. I didn't think I would," she shook her head in disbelief, "but I am."

Michael grinned, "You do know this is a long term commitment?" He wiped her cheek with an even muckier finger.

"Is that the garden you're talking about?" she smiled, "or us?"

Daffodils and crocuses gave way to fuchsias and roses. Gayle changed, too. By the middle of summer, her long nails had been trimmed short, and a scattering of freckles covered her shoulders and nose. She began most days now by walking round the garden, mug of tea in hand, checking for any new blooms, and daring a weed to appear. Always, the sweet scent of honeysuckle wafted over the garden.

"I've some news." Michael looked unusually serious. "Rob's aunt has decided to sell Honeysuckle Cottage."

Gayle drew a sharp breath, then said, "I don't suppose …"

"I thought you didn't do country?" he grinned.

"Honeysuckle Cottage is ours." Michael's voice danced across the garden. "At least," he went on, "it will be, in about twenty five years' time."

"Good." Gayle squinted up from the border she was weeding, "I have plans for the next twenty five years."

"Plans?" Michael knelt down beside her, absentmindedly lifting a handful of rich soil and letting it trickle through his fingers. "What plans?"

"Next spring," she pointed with her trowel, "I'm going to plant something in the shade of the oak tree." She smiled. "It's the perfect spot."

Michael frowned. "I'm not so sure about that," he brought all his months of gardening experience to the fore, "what with the shade and the roots underneath…" he paused, puzzled at Gayle's laughter.

She grabbed his arm and pulled him to his feet. "The perfect thing to plant in the shade of the oak tree next year," she took a deep breath, "would be a pram."

"A pram?" She could almost see Michael's mind flicking through all their new gardening books trying to find this particular plant. Then it clicked. "A pram!" He turned. "Are you sure?"

She nodded. "The doctor confirmed it this morning. I think we're finally putting down our own roots in Honeysuckle Cottage."

Birthday Girl
by Lesley Deschner

Martin was on a health kick and rabbit food just didn't hit the spot. 'The Oak' served food 'til closing – handy when you're fighting off a bug that makes you sleep for two days, and then wake up at 11pm, ravenous.

The pub was busy but not crowded, despite the 18th birthday party going on in the lounge. A young woman's laughter caught his attention and he smiled, noticing that the 'Birthday Girl' sash she was wearing appeared to cover more of her than her outfit. She was pretty – and pretty drunk, being supported by two of her pals who were only slightly less intoxicated. Martin couldn't keep his eyes off her and, as she staggered past him giggling, the sparkling blue of hers met the deep hazel of his.

Mustering as much composure as her state would allow, she looked Martin square-ish in the eye and said, "Hiya, handsome!" Composure collapsed in a fit of giggles and the friends quickly ushered 'Birthday Girl' off, leaving Martin's broad grin behind. A fierce spasm gripped his gut and he clutched his stomach. It eased just as abruptly, quickly followed by another. That bloody burger!

Martin was rid of the burger but the terrible hunger was back. He turned for home, walking right into 'Birthday Girl', alone. She pressed against him, smiling. In the alleyway, hands exploring, lips tasting, savouring, the hunger increased. As her limp body slid to the ground, drained of her life's blood, Martin's hunger was finally satisfied.

Framed
by Helena Sheridan

"I didn't do it," John insisted. "I swear."

Inspector Kelly cast a suspicious glance towards John's blood-stained shirt. "Well, she sure as hell didn't stab herself," he said with conviction.

John winced at the insensitive comment. He had to be careful. Kelly was shrewd. One hint of his involvement in the crime and all would be lost.

Kelly stooped to take charge of the weapon in his gloved hands. The slender gold blade of the ornate letter opener glistened under the artificial light.

Feigning distress, John slumped into a nearby chair. He cupped his head in his hands and muttered regret. It was an award winning performance, he thought. Kelly was sure to be convinced. Through his partially-opened fingers, he could still see Miriam lying on the carpet. A jagged gash scored her slender neck. Her violet dress had been ripped beyond recognition by the savage attack.

"Nasty business," Kelly said, observing the scene.

John glanced up briefly. He fought to suppress the excitement which swept over him. This was the moment he had been waiting for. He assumed a suitably tortured expression. "Why did he do it?" he moaned.

Kelly stopped and raised an inquisitive eyebrow. Slowly he drew a notebook from his top pocket. "What's that?"

Remembering his role, John shook his head. Years of sibling rivalry surged within him. He longed to implicate his younger brother, but to blurt out a vindictive response with ease may seem suspicious. Instead he threw a pleading look towards the Inspector. He shrugged, as if wrestling with a difficult moral decision. Kelly sighed. Impatiently, he tapped his pen, ready to note the slightest revelation.

"It was my brother, Tom," John dragged out the admission at last. "I knew he always wanted Miriam, but never thought he would do...*this*."

Kelly's pen skimmed across the page as he eagerly accepted John's contrived evidence.

"He was jealous?" Kelly ventured a motive for the offence.

John nodded and, taking another laboured breath, added, "He had hoped to end up with Miriam himself, you see, but when I got her, well, he just flipped."

He bit hard into his trembling lips. A nice touch, he congratulated himself. Revenge was sweet. Kelly seemed persuaded.

If questioned, Tom could not dispute his admiration for Miriam. They had both loved her from that very first encounter at Aunt Mary's dinner party. John sighed at the memory. To think he had initially invented a lame excuse to avoid the function. The lure of a 'sure thing' at the track had seemed far more exhilarating than his aunt's incessant prattle about the 'good old days'.

Thank goodness he had reconsidered offending the wealthy relative. Armed with a huge bunch of flowers and an equally flowery apology, he had arrived late. It was then he had caught sight of Miriam.

Close to a small leaded window, just off the main hall, she was bathed by a shaft of sunlight. Her soft chestnut hair tumbled provocatively across her milky white shoulders. Instantly his heart had warmed to her tantalising half smile and the mysterious sparkle in her hazel eyes.

Aunt Mary had been quick to note his interest. "What do you think?" she whispered, "Gorgeous, isn't she? Tom's quite taken with her too." Her casual remark had gripped him with a wild possessiveness that rekindled their rivalry.

Yet, despite Tom's intense fight to win, he had got Miriam. John gazed down at her disfigured face. Pity it had all ended so senselessly.

"And the letter opener?" Kelly's gruff voice summoned John back to reality. "Is it yours?"

"No, it's Tom's. My aunt left it to him in her will." He allowed his voice to dwindle effectively. "She died suddenly, a month ago."

The evidence planted, John paused to invent a cover story.

"Tom came round here this evening. He'd been drinking and was pretty fired up. He saw Miriam and...I tried to stop him, but..." He gestured weakly. "There was nothing I could do."

Kelly mulled over his version of the facts. If only he knew the truth, John thought. It was quite a different story.

His mind returned to the actual visit he had made to Tom's apartment that evening and to their hostile clash.

"I'm not paying your gambling debts, you scrounger!" Tom had sharply rejected his plea for funds. "It's your problem. You get out of it!"

He had been furious at Tom's self-righteous attitude. It was inevitable that their heated words would erupt into a bloody exchange of blows. If only Aunt Mary had been alive. She would have given him a loan. He cursed the financial situation that had forced him towards the loathsome plan.

It had been easy to extract the letter opener from Tom's desk. The incriminating evidence was necessary if his scheme was to work. John gripped his hands tightly, haunted by the image of the finely honed blade striking madly at Miriam's innocent face.

Kelly rested a supportive hand on his shoulder and tapped his brow thoughtfully. If he would just say something, John thought, let him know where he stood. He could barely stand the tension. Everything rested on the Inspector's decision...

"Well, Mr Gardiner," Kelly started slowly, "I sympathise with your loss."

"She was very special," John remembered to appear distraught.

Kelly continued to flick through the papers. "And although this dreadful business does not appear to be your fault, Mr Gardiner, sadly there's nothing I can do. I see the policy lapsed yesterday," the insurance inspector told him. "I'm sorry to say you won't get a penny!"

John moaned with genuine despair. He would never have made such a sacrifice had there been any other way, but the terms of Aunt Mary's will were precise. Tom was to get the valuable letter opener while he acquired Miriam – a priceless painting. Now he had destroyed this most treasured thing – and for what? He'd been so close, so close…

Nightfall
by Catherine Lang

Peter took one last look at the image on his phone as he sprinted for the car. Even on the tiny screen the picture was unmistakable. Jenny's naked body was all too visible, and even from the back anyone, especially his wife Mary, would recognise the livid scar on his shoulder that was testament to her fiery temper.

Mary's devotion was absolute but so was her jealous nature. He bought her forgiveness the last time with a promise never to stray again. But then Jenny had come along, with her willing body. How could he resist?

He'd been so careful but Jenny's treacherous demand for £100,000 had left him speechless.

"Come on, Peter. You don't think I wanted you for your flabby belly and bald head? This is just small change to you."

"Small change? She'd know if I took that much. I need more time."

She'd given him a week but when he failed to keep his promise Jenny had just smiled and pressed the send button.

"You deserve all you'll get. She'll destroy you this time."

He drove into the night, those terrible words ringing in his ears. He had to face Mary, to explain, to beg forgiveness, to soften her anger.

He crept into the house, silently closing the door; it seemed to shut with a resounding crash.

Turning, he saw Mary standing in the hall, her arms outstretched. Maybe she hadn't seen the message. He still had a chance.

"I've missed you," she said, and fired again.

Clearances
by Greta Yorke

Crofts in the Highlands
lie lonely and bare
each one of them ravaged
and left in despair,
ruined by wind, by frost and by rain
and man, don't forget, bears the brunt of the blame.
Nobody lives there now, all of them fled,
chased out from their homes and the lives they had led
each one of them victim of power and of greed
scattered abroad like a thistledown seed.

Imitation of Life
by Lesley Deschner

Sunlight heralded the day,
and chased the image of you away.
I struggled hard to bring it back,
but my efforts were in vain.

I wanted so to see your face,
laughing, happy, at home and safe.
Perhaps if I could conjure it,
I could keep away the pain.

Another image came to me –
the one I didn't want to see.
Your face, last seen, so cold, so still.
My tears fell down like rain.

Tongue-Tied
by Fiona Atchison

He squinted at the computer screen in order to get a better look and wondered if he dare enter the online chat room. Suddenly the front door slammed shut and a female voice called to him from the hallway. If she found him using the computer again at this time of day, she would start to get suspicious. As quickly and silently as possible he closed the screen down. Her head swung round the door "Okay dear? Sorry I'm late. I'll just put the tea on – got your favourite."

His mind quickly conjured up the image of two small plastic bags, each containing a partial human tongue. And at this present time, they were languishing in the freezer.

He nodded with a smile and gave her the thumbs up.

DCI Joyce Stokes showered quickly, cursing the fact she would be late on her first day back at the station. The honeymoon in Paris had been wonderful, but now it was back to rainy Glasgow. She caught the tail end of Trevor Parker's comment as she walked to her desk, "...looking a bit the worse for wear, eh boys?"

As Joyce drew Trevor a contemptuous glare she was aware of the stout figure of DI Tom Baxter standing in front of the crime board, eager to get started.

"Okay everyone, let's have some shush can we? Last night a young man, now identified as Joss White, was found dead in an alleyway off Renfield Street. As you can see from the photographs, the cause of death appears to be from the number of stab wounds to his back and," Baxter paused, "there's something else – half his tongue was missing. That's the same MO as Jim Mackay four weeks ago, who was found on the floor of his tenement close in Easterhouse. He'd suffered multiple stab wounds to his back, and his tongue had been partially removed. Same cause of death, which means, lads and lassies – get me some answers before the press have a field day."

"So, are you saying it could be the same killer, boss? A serial killer like?" Trevor asked.

"Let's look for some evidence first shall we? It may be a possibility or perhaps it's a copycat kill from the papers' cover of the first murder." Tom glared around the room. "Just let's pray the leads from this corpse don't go as cold as the last."

He felt a release of tension today. She had decided to visit her mum, in Paisley and he could use the time to plan. He peered through a gap in the blind, out the living-room window. The car was gone. He double-checked: yes the front door was locked. Back in his bedroom his heart thumped hard as he entered an online chat room. He started to type: 'You don't know why Mackay and White are dead, but I do. This is a warning, to the police – leave well alone and no one else will get hurt.'

When Joyce got back home around 7.30pm she found husband Chris in the kitchen reading the paper. "Hi love," he said reaching for her. This was the part of the day she liked best, curling up on the settee with Chris, a glass of red wine, and the aroma of a casserole wafting from the oven. She settled down and began to rethink her findings of the day.

There had been a breakthrough. Joyce had interviewed several of Joss White's social work colleagues, trying to source any similarities or contact between White and Mackay. She grimaced. The murders were now known locally as the 'double dram murders' because of a popular blend of whisky labelled Whyte & Mackay.

White was a student social worker in his final year on placement with Glasgow City Council. His supervisor, Rae Brown, and colleagues were shocked at his death. The six cases he'd been working on were currently being scrutinised by the police, but it was proving hard to find any probable connection to Mackay.

They knew Jim Mackay was 28, single and a loner, who'd had various jobs. None seemed to last longer than a year or so. He'd some previous form stealing and driving cars as a teenager. His latest stint was with the Volunteer Drivers' Association (VDA), working for mileage rates. So far it didn't look as if the victims' paths had met, but the possibility factor niggled at Joyce. The list of Mackay's pick-ups for the previous three months had been investigated and found to consist of school runs to Special Schools. Despite hard police work, there were no leads.

"Are you sure Joss has not had *some* contact with the VDA, through another colleague perhaps?" Joyce persisted, questioning his supervisor again.

Rae rubbed her eyes tiredly for a moment or two, then suddenly perked up. "Wait a minute, staff have to take a turn at 'duty', which means technically Joss could receive calls from anyone." She walked over to a desk and slowly began to turn the pages of an A4 book. Rae's voice was almost a whisper as she looked up at Joyce in alarm. Her finger pointed to a line in the book. "Oh God! He *did* make a call to the Volunteer Drivers' Centre. According to this entry about a month ago, 3rd September."

"Can you tell who the transport was ordered for and at what time?" Joyce's voice was quick and sharp with anticipation. She knew the date of the request to be only two days before Jim Mackay was found murdered.

Rae punched out a reference number from the log into her computer, and a name appeared – 'Daniel Hart'. Tapping a few more keys, a file of case notes appeared on the screen. Rae scrolled down, "Joss arranged transport for this 21-year-old man, who apparently required to attend a hospital appointment last month. He's a wheelchair user. Previous road traffic accident, three years ago according to this."

It had been a shock that the volunteer driver, Jim, had recognised him. He had no recollection of the actual accident at all, just waking up in hospital without being able to feel his legs. But, worst of all, finding he could no longer talk, or more importantly, no longer sing. He could only vaguely remember his past life. A life when he was 18 years old, able-bodied and on his way to the airport early one morning to catch a flight. He'd been accepted to study at The London School of Music. That very day instead of his life just beginning, it had sickeningly ended.

DC Trevor Parker was bursting with news for Joyce and the DI. He'd questioned the VDA driving co-ordinator again, who remembered the regular afternoon driver for 3rd September had failed to turn in. Mackay just happened to be in the office at that time. White had phoned in on spec and asked for a driver at short notice. Daniel Hart's mother had made the request. Apparently she hadn't felt well enough to drive him to the hospital herself as she usually did.

"The absentee driver's name was still entered in their book for that afternoon." Parker explained. "But it was our victim, Mackay, who actually did the run. The entry was never corrected."

Baxter's small frame sprang into action. "Right, get over quickly to Daniel Hart's address. This new information links White and Mackay – a lead we missed first time round."

It had been a surreal conversation, Daniel recalled, and one sided. Jim Mackay, the guy sent round from the Volunteer Drivers' Centre, had recognised him straight away. He'd actually confessed to being the other driver involved in his accident! Mackay told Daniel he'd felt really guilty and followed events in the newspaper. He'd explained to him how upset he'd been on learning that Daniel was so badly injured. Sitting, unable to speak, Daniel felt a fury rise in him that he found hard to control.

Joyce and Trevor walked up the wheelchair ramp leading to Daniel Hart's front door. Trevor rapped the knocker smartly and winked at Joyce, "Hope he doesn't try to make a run for it."

"I see you passed your disability awareness training then," she replied.

The door slowly opened revealing a tall, wiry woman who smiled as they explained who they were. "Daniel's in his room at the moment. I think he may be sleeping, he gets very tired by teatime," she explained. "I'm his mother, so if I can be of any help?"

Joyce sat down on the offered chair. There was a smell of stale alcohol hanging around the room. "Mrs Hart, we believe you ordered a Volunteer Driver for your son through social services, about a month ago or so to take him to hospital?" she enquired.

"Yes, that's right, I had a migraine. I get them from time to time and can't drive. Affects my vision you see. Why are you asking?"

"The man who drove your son that day, Mrs Hart, was called Jim Mackay," Joyce replied.

"He was murdered two days later," Trevor interrupted abruptly. "The person you made the driving request to, Joss White, was also found dead, earlier this week."

Mrs Hart reached for a glass and took a small sip, "That's dreadful, those poor young men...but what's this got to do with Daniel?"

Joyce spoke softly, "Mrs Hart, does your son sometimes go out in the evenings – on his own?"

He could hear his mother's voice and that of two other people talking in the next room but couldn't make out what they were saying. He had a good idea it was the police though. She'd told him to pretend he was asleep, so he'd transferred himself from his wheelchair to bed. What was she going to say?

DI Tom Baxter sat opposite Joyce in the canteen. After a short debrief involving the visit to Daniel Hart, everyone seemed a bit deflated. The only lead they had was a young disabled man, whom they would return to try to question the next day. Apparently, he never went out of the house unaccompanied. Apart from needing to use a wheelchair, he had no speech and poor vision. Not top of the list as suspect material. Mrs Hart had given her son a cast iron alibi for the evenings in question. They were home together every night usually watching television.

On the road to the hospital Jim had started talking and it seemed he couldn't stop.

"The car came flying round a blind corner. I didn't have time to think, never mind try to avoid you. I was lucky, a few cuts, but it's a wonder we weren't all killed."

Daniel, unable to speak, had sat in shock trying to take in what he was hearing. What did Mackay mean by 'all'? In the weeks following the accident he knew that he'd been found alone in the car, a victim, supposedly of a hit and run. Had there been a passenger in Mackay's car? He wished he'd taken his 'talk-type-writer' with him to ask.

Next morning a call came into the station from the Police IT section. Baxter relayed the news. "You're not going to believe this, but a warning note regarding the killings of White and Mackay has been posted in a chat-room website and traced to Daniel Hart's computer."

"A hundred per cent sure boss?" Trevor asked.

"Well, a hundred per cent *his* computer, but maybe he's not the only one with access remember," Joyce added. She could have kicked herself for not insisting on questioning Daniel the evening before.

Fifteen minutes later, Joyce and Trevor stood knocking at the front door of Daniel Hart's house, gaining no reply.

"Let's try round the back," said Trevor.

Mackay had kept talking. "It was the woman driving your car who told me to sling my hook. She warned me she'd pin the blame on me if I said anything to the polis or anyone. And I'm sorry pal, but I didn't need telling twice. What I could never fathom out was, how come you were found alone and in the driving seat? Where did she disappear to?"

A penny suddenly clanged in Daniel's head. The vivid flashback memories he'd had after the accident were not figments of his imagination. In these dreams he could visualise his mother insisting on driving that morning. He'd tried to stop her – she'd been drinking as usual. In the end he'd thought it wasn't worth the hassle, because he would soon be away from her. Daniel felt his blood chill. His own mother had caused the accident, and then hauled him into the driver's seat and left him to his injuries.

Steps led up to a glass paned door. Through it they could see the figure of a young man slumped in his wheelchair. Trevor broke a pane of glass and put his hand inside to unlock the door.

Jim Mackay had returned Daniel home after his hospital appointment. She'd come to the door, staggering slightly as she always did during a binge. But he'd caught the look on her face as she'd stared into the eyes of Mackay. Neither said a word, but that glimpse of mutual recognition had been enough.

She'd tried to act as if everything was normal. But when he'd heard about the murder of Jim Mackay, then poor Joss White, he knew...

Entering the kitchen, Joyce nearly fell over the prone body of Mrs Hart, lying in a pool of congealed blood. On searching the house, forensics made the grisly discovery of two severed tongues, now undergoing DNA testing. The young disabled man was being questioned at the station. He had an advocate with him, and answered questions using a talk-type-writer. As his story unfolded, Joyce listened incredulously. A bitter, alcoholic woman had almost killed her son, and then murdered two innocent young men three years later thinking she was keeping her awful secret from him. Mackay had been killed because he had recognised her. Joss White's only crime had been to order a volunteer driver for her son. She couldn't take the risk but, ironically, killing White had led the police straight to her. They could only guess why she had severed her victims' tongues – a symbol perhaps of their silence.

His mother had started drinking heavily when the police left. He'd quietly transferred back into his wheelchair. She was drinking at the kitchen table, and tried to smile at him. "Everything's okay now, love," she slurred. "Mother's sorted it all out again."

He typed 'Why did you leave me in the car?'

She stared at him for a long, long moment then shrugged her shoulders. "I just panicked."

He made a crying sound at the back of his throat, 'You ruined my life.'

She stood up unsteadily and hissed "And what about my life, what about me? You didn't think twice about leaving me alone to go to some fancy music school." Her voice became bitter, "You almost left me, just like your father. That will never happen again."

His world became slow motion but his mind was clear as his hand reached to the cushion on his wheelchair, where he'd placed the kitchen knife.

Autumn Shades
by Fiona McFadzean

The night storm plundered the trees
to carpet the lawn, in russet and bronze,
the day you came to us.
A wriggling ball of fur, golden as the dawn,
you tunnelled through the leaves, only your
waving tail plotting your course, before you
hurled yourself towards us, with loving licks
for your new young master.
"I'll call her Saffron," Tom decided.

'Saffie' you became, a dog for all seasons,
the only constant in lives so changed
with passing years.
Last spring Tom marched a continent away,
to do his duty, playing a very different game of
chase and catch; a game that few condone,
or even understand.
It was then he felt your loss, and you his.

Now it is my turn, as another autumn comes.
Your pain-filled eyes beseech, telling it is time to let
you go. Tom's distance almost too much to bear
the day you leave us.
A gentle breeze persuades the trees to cover you,
in russet and bronze, where you lie asleep forever
in your favourite corner.
Closing my eyes I see a kaleidoscope
of boy and dog, playing their many games.
I smile through the tears.

Photographic Memory
by Catherine Lang

Beth gazes in awe at the scene before her. It's even better than she and Don could have imagined. The men stand in serried ranks, stone-faced but alert, ready to do their Captain's bidding.

"It'll be just magic, love. A great way to celebrate your 60th and my retirement," Don had said. It is certainly an amazing sight, even if it has taken a couple more years finally to achieve their goal.

Beth's eyes mist over. She blinks fiercely. She is not going to miss one moment of this spectacle – and she has her new camera to record it all too. As she peers at the view-screen she remembers the gentle voice of her instructor.

"I've taught you all I can. You know the set up backwards. Just remember, if you split the picture into thirds horizontally and vertically you'll get a better image. It's not rocket science."

But it wasn't Don who had shown her how to operate the new digital camera she held so confidently. Don had been a photographer all his life, working for the local newspaper. His cameras were his way of keeping memories fresh. He loved taking images of people and places, and every family occasion had been carefully recorded on film and meticulously archived.

He'd even managed to take some of the shots at Carol's wedding allowing their son Peter charge of the precious equipment only when his duties as father of the bride meant he had to be in the picture. Carol's wedding pictures were extra precious as, less than 10 days later, just as they had started to pour over the brochures for their trip of a lifetime, the stroke had hit him. He'd lain in a coma for only four days before he died, taking with him so much more than his presence.

The newly married Carol had been supportive but she and her husband had their own busy lives, while Peter was studying photography 200 miles away. Beth had continued with her routine automatically, no longer finding joy in each day or in contemplating the future.

She even gave up visiting the library. Before Don's death she had made a weekly pilgrimage to the local town to hear their latest speaker and to select a couple of books, usually from the romantic fiction section. She and Don had known the librarian, Ralph Sims, since school days and he had always been a great friend, keeping the latest titles by her favourite romantic authors for her if he could.

She was no longer in the mood for soppy romance, now that Don was not there to tease her as she sniffled her way through another happy ending. Too unlike the lonely life she had to face in the echoing, empty house.

Beth knew that there was another reason. Just six months after Don's death Ralph had lost his wife. Ralph had nursed Megan for a year and Beth envied them the time they had had to speak about their parting, not having it forced upon them without a moment's notice. There was so much that she should have said to the man who'd been her friend and helpmate for almost 40 years.

She had only gone back after a gap of 18 months because of Peter. He was spending his Easter vacation with her and had ordered a selection of travel books to study over the break. With Mike, his best friend, Peter was planning to disappear for three months over the summer to visit and photograph some of the more exotic locations in Europe and the Far East.

Ralph greeted Beth with his usual warmth, as if just a few weeks had passed.

"Weren't you and Don planning a trip to China for his retirement?" Ralph asked, stamping a huge book on the world's most populated country amongst the pile.

Beth just nodded, trying not to remember the excited plans that they had been making the very night before he took ill.

"I've always wanted to go, ever since I read about their history," Don had said. "Such an amazing place. It could take a lifetime to understand about it all."

"You could go with Peter, you know," suggested Ralph, breaking into her reverie.

"Don't be daft. He and Mike are going backpacking," she retorted with a grin.

"Well, lots of tour companies are going there these days. You can find them on the net."

"What net?" asked Beth, puzzled.

"The internet of course," smiled Ralph, pointing across at the ranks of colourful computer screens and their busy operators.

"Oh, Don didn't hold with all that. He said digital would be the death of decent photography, He wouldn't learn how to use a computer on principle. He bought Peter one for college but I've never been near it. I wouldn't know where to start."

"I know. He hated it when we changed the dark room here into a training suite. That was the end of the Camera Club. But even dusty old libraries have to move with the times. I'd be happy to teach you computing if you'd like," Ralph smiled.

Flicking through the book on China later that evening, Beth had felt a surge of enthusiasm she hadn't known for months. It wouldn't do any harm just to have a look at this internet to see what was available, Beth thought.

Over the next few weeks Ralph showed her the basics of computing, initially on the library equipment. After a few lessons he somewhat shyly suggested that she could learn more quickly on his home machine.

Soon Monday mornings and Thursday afternoons were spent in Ralph's recently acquired little flat, filled with dozens of framed photographs of Megan and their life together.

"Don taught me the basics of photography years ago." Ralph sighed, "His skill and enthusiasm were catching, though he hated it when I joined the digital world."

Sitting quietly over a coffee late one Thursday afternoon, when Beth had had her first foray deep into the World Wide Web to check out travel companies, she told Ralph all about her last evening with Don and why they'd planned that particular holiday.

Ralph looked intently at Beth. "It may seem a terrible thing to say I know, but I envy you the way Don went."

Beth didn't know whether to be shocked or astonished. "But he went with so much unsaid. At least you and Megan had time to talk things through."

"I suppose in that way we were blessed, but I had to watch my darling girl shrink day by day, the treatment almost worse than the disease. She'd always been so full of life but latterly I had to do everything for her, and nothing could really take away the pain. She was remarkably brave but I could see it in her eyes. In the end, all we could plan was her funeral. Don went to bed happy, full of dreams for the future, and never woke up. If Megan had to go, I've often wished it had been that quick."

Ralph wiped away a tear and Beth found herself reaching out and touching his hand with understanding.

July saw the boys set off on their Eastern adventure. Once she'd learned the intricacies of email, Ralph had set her up an email account so that she could read her mail after her lessons. Peter occasionally found an internet café and sent a message to say he was OK and that the store of photographs was steadily growing. One in particular set her thinking:

I know dad wouldn't approve, mum, but this digital stuff is really great. I've taken hundreds of photos and been able to select the best as we go! Off to Xi'an in the morning to see you know what!

He had written from Beijing where they were treating themselves to a couple of nights in a five star hotel after travelling from Moscow on the trans-Siberian railway.

"Isn't it about time you bit the bullet and booked that holiday?" asked Ralph, reading Peter's message.

Beth had to admit that the idea had been growing on her as she read more about the country and its history. Don had always said that too many people thought China came into being in 1949 and didn't like it on principle. They forgot the thousands of years of civilization before the advent of Communism, and the cultural heritage and pride that it had engendered.

So she had booked her two week trip. She even let Ralph talk her into buying a little digital camera of her own and teach her how to use it properly.

"There's a lot more to it than point and click," he had admonished, grinning.

"Peter says he has hundreds of pictures," she protested.

"You have to learn to see the world through your own eyes from now on, Beth," Ralph had said. It was a hard lesson to face up to but she knew he was right. By the time he delivered Beth and her luggage to the airport for her November trip, she was quite the expert.

"You may never be David Bailey but you'll do," was Ralph's parting shot as he kissed her cheek and left her with the tour manager.

Now she is standing alone, gazing awestruck at the Terracotta Army so painstakingly restored over the decades since its discovery by a simple farmer digging a well. She has seen the Forbidden City, walked on the Great Wall, even been to the

Great Dam, but this is what she wants to see more than anything. She and Don had learned about the detail in the figures, fascinated by the fact that 2200 years ago the craftsmen had created 8000 heads, each with completely individual features.

"We'll be able to see what the people of the time actually looked like," Don had said. "For me, each one is a photograph in fired earth, restored despite rebellion and earthquake for us to marvel at and learn from."

Beth feels the lump in her throat that Don isn't here to marvel at the petrified warriors with her. Yet, as she walks around, carefully taking her photographs, Beth is filled with joy at the knowledge that she has someone to share this knowledge and these fascinating images, someone to help her look again to the future. As she sets up her final shot of the kneeling archer, with his rakish topknot, the decision is made. As soon as she gets back to the hotel she will email Ralph and accept his invitation to spend Christmas with him.

And she'll make sure she has her camera with her to begin to record a new set of memories.

Ode to an Ageing Hippie
by Helena Sheridan

There was a time, not long ago, at least that's how it seems,
When life was filled with laughter and wild romantic dreams,
And I could dance forever when hopes and heels were high,
And sentimental movies were all that made me cry.
When vinyl records made the charts and kaftans were the rage,
I'd followed every fashion in that psychedelic age.
But now my era's ended and I think it's kind of sad,
I once was 'cool' but now I'm cold; my circulation's bad,
With discs disintegrating, my disco days are through,
The only date I get is when my BP check is due.
I didn't need a Bus Pass when I used to take a 'trip',
Or get a hip replacement to make this hippie hip,
And as for flower power, it's primrose oil these days,
And 'peace and love's' forgotten when the family comes to stay.
But when the youngsters laugh at me, one thought I find sublime,
In just a few short years they'll say, there used to be a time…

True Love
by Janice Johnston

Click, click.

I fell in love with her that very first day in the park, but you don't want to blurt out something like that immediately. She sparkled in the sunshine, kicking through the leaves and laughing when she thought no-one was looking. From a distance, it was just like one of those pictures you see on calendars, the huge oak trees framed her perfectly. For a moment I'd hesitated about taking photos, you never can capture that sheer joy. It's so fleeting you have to suck it in at that very moment. It made me feel happy and fulfilled and, I suppose, joyful as I watched her.

I checked on the photos I'd taken already. The distance shots were good but the close-ups - even on the camera's small screen - were perfect. Somehow she'd managed to squeeze life and love through the lens. I couldn't wait to blow up the images for my wall.

It was then that I knew. She was my One True Love.

It was good to feel like that again. For a long while - well, since Lyndsay, if you must know - life had been so flat. I felt like a cardboard cut-out in a black and white montage - the rest of the world only moved by jerking along in the corners of my eyes. Now, with Julia in my life - Julia, that's her name - I could see all the autumn colours dancing.

Click, click.

I walked Julia home that first day. She stays in one of those apartments just across from the park.

Not one of the expensive ones facing on to the park, you understand, but an apartment on one of the side roads. It's still a nice area.

A nice area for a nice girl.

Lyndsay wasn't a nice girl. She never appreciated my devotion, even after everything I had done for her. I was going to say she never appreciated my love, but now I know I never truly loved Lyndsay. Not once I'd met Julia.

The next day, I left Julia her first little surprise. I set off early, before any of the joggers or dog walkers would see me. Her street was quiet, clean, as I approached her door. The railings outside were the perfect place to tie her huge silver balloon, white letters spelling out, 'I love you, Julia' for all to see.

She found it as she left for work. She laughed and looked round, trying to spot me. I stayed hidden, hugging her joy to me.

Click, click.

That was the best time, the first time I left a gift. She was so fresh, so open, so innocent in those photos.

When she found my other presents – always wrapped in silver paper – she didn't laugh any more. She picked them up carefully and carried them inside, all the better to savour the unwrapping, the anticipation, the thought behind the gift. But she kept her head down and didn't look round to try and catch sight of me.

Not like Lyndsay. No, I shouldn't think about Lyndsay, she can still upset me. At the end, she would stand on her doorstep and tear my carefully chosen and beautifully wrapped gifts into shreds.

Lyndsay smashed the little figurine I'd chosen for her and stamped on the wooden box – no, I didn't like that. And she yelled. Horrible, hurtful, untrue things.

Click, click.

Afterwards, when I looked, those photos showed rage and hate, not the feistiness and individuality that had drawn me to her.

The phone calls to Lyndsay turned nasty, too. Her so-called friends turned her against me. She screamed and shouted on the phone – then she cried. I didn't like making her cry. Next time I called the number it was unobtainable.

I had to wait outside her apartment for hours, it felt like days, before I caught up with her. Maybe it was days.

Click, click.

That's when things started to go black and white.

After, I moved away from her neighbourhood but it was a while before I felt things were back to normal. Not until I fell in love with Julia in the park that autumn day.

I wonder what Lyndsay did with my love letters?

I expected Julia to keep hers in a special box, maybe covered with silver paper from one of my presents. That's the sort of romantic thing I thought she would do. But any time I was in Julia's apartment I never saw them. Mind you, I didn't like to rummage through all her secret places. I just opened her drawers and wardrobe and smelt her smell. I was very careful not to move anything. She's a very tidy girl, Julia. I only wanted to be a bigger part of her life.

Click, click.

That's why I phoned so much, too. She has a lovely voice, Julia, sweet and singing and happy. Lately though, I've noticed it's more strained, higher, sharper. She's doing too much at work, I'm sure. Her voicemail voice is always sweet, though, 'I'm sorry I can't come to the phone right now. Please leave your message after the tone.' Not that I ever leave a message – I don't like talking to machines – but sometimes I phone two, three, even more times to hear her voice.

Click, click.

Tonight, I walk Julia home from work, as usual. I have another little surprise for her, wrapped in silver paper and tucked under my jacket so she won't see it too soon and spoil the surprise. It's an ice-blue scarf, to match her eyes and her navy jacket. I've noticed she's looking peaky and has lost weight; I don't want her to become ill.

At the door she fumbles with the key then takes a breath and turns to smile at me before pushing the door open and quickly closing it behind her.

I begin smiling in anticipation of the joy on her face when she finds my gift. I wish she would laugh again but that hasn't happened for a while now.

I wait. Teasing her. Letting her reach the door of her apartment before ringing her bell. I pull out her present and drop it on the doorstep, turning to leave and watch her from my usual spot.

But white lights blind me. Black shadows, figures, move in the corner of my eyes. Voices shouting again – about Lyndsay. But Lyndsay is black and white now, all the goodness and joy sucked out.

Click, click.

I carry the snapshot in my mind of the last time I saw her. Her bedroom. Her body. Black and white. And red.

Batch Baker
by Fiona Atchison

The first therapy I responded to was baking. Mixing, kneading, whisking, all miraculously worked to de-steam me to a controllable level. So now I batch bake, every day, churning out cakes and pastries for the wards.

One year gone, no straitjacket needed and joy of joy, my twin, Lionel is being allowed to visit today. Not mother though. Not yet.

She never let me bake at home. "*Lily!*" she'd shriek, "get out of this kitchen."

Guess who always got the spoon to lick? Lionel! Not that I minded because mother's cake mixes were vile. Unlike mine. My pastries are so light they melt in the mouth, everyone says so.

I've baked Lionel's favourite. Lemon meringue pie. It's already sliced because I'm not allowed a knife.

"Looking good, Lily," is the first thing he says. But I'm not sure if he means me as his eyes are on the pie. Makes a change. I tremble with anger, remembering how he used to stare at me, then touch...

The nurse motions her head smilingly, so I pour the tea and proffer some pie to Lionel. Fussy me scrapes off the meringue on mine. I tell Lionel about my baking therapy and my art therapy too, of course. Mosaics of coloured glass.

I cut and grind the glass very, very carefully, the remnants of which I used in the meringue.

Only no-one knows that part.

Well, not yet.

Pageant Day
by Fiona McFadzean

I open the window to let a breath of air into the room and get a blast of music from the PA system in the distant park. The slight breeze isn't enough to make the multi-coloured bunting dance to its beat. I know the feeling. I am as limp as it looks. The weather forecast did promise a scorcher of a day, but how often can we rely on 'them' getting it right? It is cooler here at the front of the house and I sit down on the window seat, just for a minute.

The front door opposite opens and two teenagers catapult onto the pavement. They high five each other and shout "Yes". When they catch sight of me, the older one calls across "Great day for it, isn't it?"

Then the younger one adds, "We're off to meet our friends, we're all going to…"

Before she can say any more her sister cuts in, "Come on," and pulls at her arm.

"Enjoy yourselves," I call after them as they march off, mobile phones very much in evidence although it has to be said that their skirts are not. I lean back, close my eyes and think of another two girls. Girls clad in flowery summer dresses, not skirts shorter than shorts and skimpy T shirts that barely cover their modesty.

Bunting, crowds, music. Excitement almost tangible. Brilliant sunshine a bonus. The town square and the road leading to the park are awash with folks dressed in their best. Maggie and I are on our own, with no minders watching our every move. It had taken much promising and cajoling to make it happen. In the end Granny proved to be our greatest ally, much to our surprise. "Let them go," she told our parents. "I know that they won't do anything that I wouldn't do." We smiled at that. Great Aunt Amy, after one gin too many, had once shared a bit of granny's risqué past. We reckoned that gave us a bit of scope. As for the promise that we would stick together? Don't we always!

We walk towards the Park, skipping on and off the pavement as if we were five again instead of almost third years at High School. "Let's wait here for the Parade," Maggie says as we reach a good vantage point for seeing the Queen's carriage and all the decorated floats pass by.

"Good idea," I answer, "shouldn't be long now."

"I can't wait to see His Nibs," Maggie utters, before choking on one of her crisps.

I look at her red face and thump her on the back while telling her "I'll bet his face is as red as yours, he will be roasting in his costume in this heat." She continues to scoff her crisps. I know exactly who she means. His Nibs, two years older than us, lives in the house between mine and Maggie's. He has been the bane of our lives for as long as I can remember – pulled pigtails, frogs in the wrong places, and so on. Much to his disgust, and our delight, he was chosen to be Consort to the Pageant Queen. And, today's the Day he gets to wear that costume. "With him as her consort God will definitely have to save the Queen," I mutter, making Maggie giggle again.

"Here it comes," someone shouts. Necks crane in a Mexican wave. Maggie sighs over the meringue that is Queen Julia while I split my sides laughing at the sight of her consort. Scarlet britches, gold embroidered tunic, large plumed hat. "Oh my God! What a sight!"

I don't realise that I have spoken aloud until Maggie answers, "But he does look good in it with his dark hair."

What? Has she gone soft or something?

As the carriage draws level I mince along beside it and grin at him. He glares back. Wait a minute. What is he up to? Leaning over he picks a rose from the Royal posy, throws it at me, then blows me a kiss. The Swine. I'm supposed to be making fun of him, not the other way round. Queen Julia elbows his ribs. His cronies, the Patterson twins, are standing on the opposite pavement, their ginger locks glinting in the sunshine. They'll never get lost in a fog, that's for sure. They give him a raucous cheer and a thumbs up. Maggie walks forward, picks up the rose and hands it to me. She has a peculiar expression on her face. All of a sudden I feel my cheeks growing as red as the flower and I can no longer look at her.

Instead I watch my finger caress the velvet petals. My tummy flutters. When I look up I see that the Patterson twins have joined Maggie. She walks off with Sam. Tom waits for me. I...

The sound of the front door opening jerks me to my feet and back to the reality of a very different Pageant Day for me.

"Well, that's her delivered in one piece," my husband informs me, as he aims the car keys at the wooden bowl on the sideboard.

I don't need to utter the words "Don't throw them," because our sons chorus it for me, their hands on their hips. All four of us laugh, although my husband's eyes are anxious as he looks at me. "I'm fine," I answer his unspoken question. "And, I'll be even finer when I see our daughter being crowned Pageant Queen, even if I do have to watch from the car. You did get permission to park near the platform, didn't you?"

No.1 Son answers for him. "But, you won't have to..." is as far as he gets before his brother claps a hand over his mouth and hisses, "It's a secret, Dumbo."

I know not to ask about secrets although I can't help wondering...

I sit back down on the window seat as the other three thud upstairs to get ready. On their return they will have transformed into a Piper and two Drummer Boys. The boys have inherited their father's musical talent. This will be their second parade. All three, plus my daughter, will be in the Procession – while I sit in the car. My chest, at least the half I have left, tightens.

Before I can feel extra sorry for myself the front door opens and a voice shouts "Surprise, surprise! It's not Cilla Black. It's..."

"Maggie," I squeal with delight, "what are you doing here?" The tears blind me as she sits down beside me and takes my hands.

"Away, you old softie," her voice is gruff. "Don't we always do Pageant Parade together?"

In the twinkling of an eye the house is empty except for the two of us. It will soon be time for the Parade to start from the end of our street and I look for the car keys, forgetting for a minute that I'm not driving today.

Maggie understands. She bursts out laughing, which I think is strange, before pointing to the hall and announcing in a posh voice, "Your carriage awaits you, Ma'am." I can't believe what I see. A wheelchair, decorated to the nines, a notice on the back proclaiming 'Queen Mum'. Once we have both donned outrageous hats I take my seat. Before we set off she touches my shoulder and whispers. "The chemo is only a formality, Annie, it will be alright."

It is my turn for the posh voice. "Please get going, lackey; one has a procession to join."

As we travel along, Maggie hops off and on the pavement enough for both of us, managing to control the chair at the same time. We don't care if anybody is watching as we giggle as if we were five again, instead of forty-something. Stopping for breath, she asks, "Do you remember the Pageant when him next door was the Queen's consort?" When I nod she continues, "And how we both had the hots for him until he made fun of you with the rose stunt." Not quite how I have been remembering it but I nod again. "To think we met our future husbands that day." She gets all dreamy. "Although we didn't know it at the time." Her sentiment deserts her and she howls with laughter. "Mind you, we would have been horrified if we had known." We chant together "because the last thing you and I ever wanted was to have carrot haired kids"

As we reach the end of the street we are adults again. Just as we were when the Patterson twins returned from Uni: the year when Maggie and I began to dream about cute babies with ginger hair.

The Pipe Band is in formation, ready to go. Tom and Sam wave to us before tuning up. My boys – not twins but a year apart – trying to be cool, ignore us. Maggie's daughter comes towards us, a huge grin on her face. She winks at her Mum and says to me, "Uncle Tom asked me to give you this." She hands me a rose. A yellow rose with a blush of pink. I know that it has been taken from the Royal Posy. A warmth that has nothing to do with the heat of the sun spreads through me. Unlike another rose on another Pageant Day, this one is full of meaning.

Final Move
by Fiona Atchison

With careless hands they wash and wipe
All dignity away, then prod and pull
Without regard for who she is, or was
Her finer features undisclosed
To those who will not stop to pause

And then they guide her to a chair,
Where she may sit and droop and stare.

For visitors the time drags long
A duty done in stifling warmth
With smells of fetid food and age
Low murmurs stumble round the room
In cloistered constraints of a cage

And as they stand to kiss goodbye,
She bravely smiles and does not cry.

Routine replays each waking hour
A pendulum of passing time
Dull eyes gaze but cannot see
From out the circle of decline
Lost in a sombre reverie

And when they say how well life seems,
She feels the rise of silent screams.

As independence slowly fades
So does the fervent hope of home
The talk of a return some day

Seemed to be a trick, a ploy
To cast the burden well away

And now they joke to humour her,
While she relents without demur.

With each day fumbling over next
Long weeks decay to months
Cocooned inside a sealed domain
A muddle minded world begins
Where she recalls her youth again

And so with protests left unsaid
She meekly walks wherever led.

Sauce for the Goose
by Catherine Lang

The noises became louder but no clearer. Laura struggled to drag herself to wakefulness. She shouldn't be asleep just now. Trying to roll over, she felt the covers heavy on her legs – that lazy cat again. Tentatively she opened her eyes and quickly shut them. It was pitch dark. She stretched out her hand, searching for the small bedside clock. It had to be there. The scream rose in her throat but died to a cough, as her open mouth filled with dust.

John stepped out of the shower. Hot water followed by the luxury of fresh towels and hot coffee. It was Sunday and he could do whatever he liked. Laura had had him working 18-hour days for the past three months. After all the negotiating and the worry, he deserved to spoil himself. For now he would do whatever he liked – and today he liked to do nothing but cook. Wrapped in his ample bathrobe he ambled to the kitchen, poured a coffee and looked out over the river, to the conurbation beyond. For this one day the clamour was shut out. The work was complete. He had earned his tranquillity.

Laura was deafened by the thunder of blood, her breath coming faster than a sprinter's. Why was she here? Where was here? Her head lay on a pillow of shattered wood, her legs blanketed by something rigid and increasingly heavy. She strained to control rising panic. There had to be a coherent explanation. Was this a nightmare? No, she was too cold and too frightened. This was real. Her accountant's mind started to click in. Once she understood what had happened everything would be fine. Wouldn't it?

John stretched lazily, slipping Beethoven's Egmont into the quadraphonic system and luxuriating in the sound. Laura should have learned to chill – she'd been so tense during these past days. Having her do his business plan had helped his credibility with the banks but he'd really just wanted Laura as a sleeping partner. He frowned at the thought! She was definitely not his type – far too pernickety. He needed his creative freedom. Never mind, once the river barge restaurant was established with its promised exclusive clientele there would be no stopping him. It was light years from the corner café he'd been brought up in, where he'd watched his mother's creative spirit fade and die in the deep fat fryer. But her passion for perfection lived in him.

Laura strained to hear any sound above the beating of her heart. Nothing. No voices, no sirens, nobody nearby. She was completely alone. She had always been alone, till Robin. Laura's heart leapt. Robin would be looking for her. The tears of relief streaming down her grimy cheeks turned to tears of despair. How would Robin know where to find her? She tried to pull herself free but an intense pain shot through her body and everything went black.

Dressed in his whites, John started to prepare the celebration lunch he had promised he'd create. A special meal for a special person. It would take time to prepare, but cooking was his life. He had willingly put in the interminable hours to hone his skills. He made a name for himself, working in other people's kitchens, preparing other men's creations, but he longed for autonomy. That's why he'd planned the restaurant. The beautiful old barge was just perfect for the type of clients they had in mind. A lot of business-people would pay handsomely for excellent cuisine in superb but secluded surroundings. Where was more secluded than a barge meandering between moorings? If only Laura hadn't kept complaining about rising estimates, trying to cut corners. Well, it was too late to change anything.

Laura returned reluctantly to wakefulness. She felt chilled. Her back was wet. Blood? No, it was too cold. She was lying in water. But how? The last thing she remembered was John's blithe comment that they were finally ready for the opening. Laura winced at the memory. They were far from ready. All the last minute additions had pushed the already shaky finances right to the edge. They'd need an amazing launch to make even the first month's repayments. Yet John didn't seem to care.

John heard his phone bleep for the third time. He should have turned it to silent. He pulled the tiny handset from the depths of his briefcase and flipped it open. He knew who was calling: the same person who had been in touch every day for the last month. Courtney - a very hands-on investor. He felt a shiver as he read the message. It was all Laura's doing. She just couldn't understand why he had to have the best of everything in his restaurant, no matter what. Now his dreams were within his grasp. And the cost? He'd pay, and willingly.

Laura was drifting, dreaming of Robin's melodious voice. She felt safe when they were together, walking by the river or relaxing in Robin's tiny waterside cabin where they had spent their too few nights together. Love at first sight wasn't a Hollywood fantasy. They'd met at the remote lochan where Laura let herself escape now and then. Robin seemed fanatical about fishing. Laura didn't really understand this passion – there never seemed to be any fish – but she loved Robin and that was enough.

John remembered the first time he met Courtney. He and Laura had been enjoying a well-earned drink at the local champagne bar. At least, he had been enjoying it. Laura, as always, had been counting the cost in money and in time. At least for once she had not voiced her complaint. She'd been mesmerised by the much brasher celebration at the neighbouring table, her eyes even larger than usual behind her heavy-rimmed spectacles. John knew Courtney by reputation – a self-made millionaire with a no nonsense attitude. A wayward champagne cork hit John's glass, tipping the contents over Laura's skirt. Scarlet with embarrassment, Laura headed for the door. Courtney had beckoned to John to join them, and the future took a on a very different face.

Laura felt Robin's kiss on her forehead. "Come on, sleepy head. It's a beautiful day and we've got to get rid of those wrinkles. Maybe the only way is to rid you of that partner of yours and his profligate spending. I have my contacts, you know!" Drifting, Laura smiled at the bravado and wriggled deeper. Pain shot through her body. The warmth of Robin's kiss faded in that instant. She was in the dark again, alone, afraid.

John had been surprised that Courtney accepted his invitation to a private lunch. The entrepreneur, who owned an international security company, was a reputed gourmand who knew his reputation but, even so, John had not expected a yes, at least not at the first attempt. He had carefully planned the menu, balancing colours, textures, flavours, to create a feast for all the senses. The outcome had been even more effective than he had hoped. He and Courtney had spent many hours eating, drinking, talking. John had found himself revealing his mother's unfulfilled passion for cooking, his own dream of turning an old river barge into an exclusive eatery, his frustration at Laura's over-cautious approach and the bank's stranglehold on his plans. Her solution had been shocking in its simplicity.

Laura tried desperately to recall Robin's touch. She imagined herself curled in the old couch in the cabin, listening to the river sounds while Robin focused on preparing the fishing gear. She'd arrived just before midnight, tired out as always. The interior seemed barer than she remembered. The ladder-back chairs were missing. Having them refurbished, Robin had said. Now Laura recalled that the little seascape was gone too. Where were Robin's favourite things?

John continued selecting his ingredients. Tomorrow would see the beginning of his new enterprise. No more bargaining with banks or fighting with Laura over equipment and running costs. Like today, all he need do was cook. Create spectacular meals for city fat cats; for anyone Courtney wanted to approach out of the public eye. The barge was an ideal setting. They had reached agreement at that very first meeting. Courtney would ensure he had everything he'd always wanted, and all he had to do was forget who enjoyed his masterpieces.

"You should cut your losses," Robin had told Laura. "Tell him you have had enough of his selfishness and you're getting out before he reduces you to a nervous wreck. You haven't invested that much money."

Laura couldn't afford to walk away. Her reputation was at stake. She tried desperately to explain. Robin had worked on the fishing basket all the time Laura was speaking, never looking her in the eye. Laura could not understand what was so fascinating about its contents or why it was taking so long to organise them.

Laura felt unsettled. It was the first time she had seen Robin angry, unreasonable, cold. As cold as she was now. Cold, but cuttingly clear-headed at last. She and Robin had sat late into the night, arguing. At 5am Robin had walked out of the cabin without a backward glance. A few moments later Laura had noticed that the fishing basket was still leaning against the door jamb. She rose, ready to run out with it into the burgeoning dawn. The sun came up in a blinding flash, the explosion of light splintering the scene.

John cursed as he heard a knock at the door. He needed at least another thirty minutes to achieve perfection. He removed his apron, folded it neatly on the counter and walked to the door. The figure on the other side looked as elegant as ever, even through the fisheye. He opened the door and was enveloped in an expensively perfumed embrace.

"It's done," said Robin's mellifluous voice. "I tried it your way but she was as stubborn as I expected. Well, now you're free of that harpy and it didn't cost a penny. We'll deal with the details tomorrow. Let's eat."

Robin Courtney draped her beautifully sculptured body on the white leather couch and smiled her enigmatic smile at John.

"You are all mine now."

The pain in Laura's legs had passed. All she could feel now was numbness. She hadn't just lost feeling in her legs. Her heart was experiencing something very similar. She knew exactly where she was and she knew that no one was going to find her.

Honeymoon in Rome
by Maggie Bolton

Dear Mum, Here's just a little line
to let you know that we are fine.
The Bridal Suite is just divine!
It's such a lovely room.
It's filled with roses, white and red,
the petals on the covers spread
on our delightful marriage bed…
shame about the groom.

We had a lovely meal last night,
romantic in the candle-light.
But David spoiled my appetite;
he moaned about the food.
The weather's lovely; nice and hot.
We've toured the area a lot.
But it spoils it all somewhat
when David's in a mood.

We saw the Forum yesterday;
buildings majestic in decay.
But David grumbled all the way.
He says they're all the same.
We saw the Colosseum too,
not that David wanted to.
He thought a better thing to do
was watch a football game.

It seemed so wonderful to me
to honeymoon in Italy.
You know I've always longed to see

'The Glory that was Rome!'
Oh Mum, there's just one little thing,
I've given David back his ring.
I've had it with this marriage thing.
I'm on the next flight home.

Teacher's Pet
by Janice Johnston

"Oh, no. Not now," I groaned, as two curious brown eyes peered through the hedge. I turned my back, clutched my paint pot, and hoped he'd go away. The picnic table I was standing on rocked ominously on the uneven ground.

My neighbour stood up and leaned forward, waiting for me to land face first in the flowerbed. When I managed to get my balance again, he sighed and finally asked the question I'd been dreading.

"Whatcha doing, Miss?"

For a moment I toyed with the idea of telling him the truth, but I knew my pedestal would crumble in seconds. I quite enjoy being hero worshipped by more than a dozen males every day, even if they are only seven years old. I couldn't risk it.

"Miss?"

My most endearing pupil was not going to give up until I gave him an answer. I drew myself up to my full height – about two and a half metres including the table – and tried to think of a reasonable explanation for me to be standing on last summer's B&Q bargain.

"I'm, erm, testing to see how strong this table is." A bit pathetic, I know, but it was the best I could come up with on a rather cold and damp April evening.

My neighbour, Calum, nodded. This he could understand. Didn't he regularly test the strength of his bed, high branches, the roof of the garden shed –

much to his mum's annoyance? Before I could stop him, he climbed up beside me and jumped enthusiastically.

"That's enough testing here, Calum." I grabbed him. "Why don't you check underneath?"

"OK." He squirmed away then pointed to the pot in my hand. "Are you going to paint it orange?"

"It's not orange, it's 'Arabian Sunset'," I said, staring at the empty pot. It was at this point I realised that dollops of paint were dripping off various parts of my body and a trail of paint led from the kitchen door to the table I was now standing on.

"Aren't you coming down, too?" Calum asked.

"No!" I looked for a reason to stay on the table. "I think this bit of wood is loose."

"My big cousin's good with wood." Calum's voice echoed eerily from under the table.

I had a vision of a spotty 14 year-old version of Calum coming to my rescue, the same dirty-blond hair flopping over those same curious eyes. I shook my head. It would be all round the village in hours and life in the classroom wouldn't be worth living.

"He's good with fires, too."

I swivelled quickly to peer at my house. Was his cousin a pyromaniac? The kitchen door banged in the wind but, apart from that, everything looked fine. Had Calum seen something – smoke, flames? The thought was almost enough to get me off the table and back into the house. Almost, but not quite.

"He let me have a go in his fire engine last week." Calum sat up beside me, swinging his legs. "He said he'd give me another go, if I found out why you were out here." He waved at his own kitchen window. A tall shadowy figure waved back.

A firefighter! Didn't they sign oaths of allegiance or vows of silence – no, maybe that was monks. Anyway, surely I could trust a firefighter not to blab. They dealt with delicate situations all the time.

I waved enthusiastically. The shadowy figure paused, but gamely waved back before making his way up the garden path.

I began to think my primary 2 girls were in for a treat if Calum grew up to look anything like his big cousin.

"Hi, I'm Mike," he smiled, "I understand you are the wonderful Miss Mitchell."

"Joanna," I gabbled from my perch. "Nice to meet you." I closed my mouth, trying to turn a drool to a smile.

Mike stood calmly, dirty blond hair flopping over those wonderful eyes, waiting. Somehow I didn't think the 'testing the strength of the table' line was going to fool him.

"This bit of wood is loose," piped up Calum.

"Yes." I said, waving my arms and making exaggerated gestures about boys with big ears.

Mike's firefighter training must include understanding weird sign language from strange females.

"OK, mate," he said, lifting Calum off the table. "Why don't you fetch your dad's claw hammer and some nails from his toolbox?"

The youngster disappeared rapidly in the direction of his house.

Mike turned back to me and smiled, "Well, what's the real reason you're standing on a table, in the garden, in the rain, with a paint pot in your hand?"

I sighed. Best get it over with. Perhaps he'd stop laughing before Calum came back. "It's a mouse."

"A mouse?" His lips trembled, but he managed to keep a straight face. "You mean the wonderful Miss Mitchell is scared of mice?"

"Just don't tell Calum," I hissed, "or I'll have a classroom full of them before you can say 'revolting rodents'."

"My lips are sealed."

I'm sure they quivered again.

"Where is it, anyway?" Mike peered under the table.

"No, not here. In the kitchen. It..." I shuddered at the memory, "it nibbled my toe."

"Ah." Mike glanced at my feet. "This orange toe?"

"It's not orange, it's 'Arabian Sunset'. I thought it would brighten up the living room."

"Well," Mike grinned, "it certainly brightens you up. Tell me, is this down to the mouse, too, or is there another reason you've poured orange..." I glared at him, "sorry, 'Arabian Sunset' paint all over yourself?"

"When I felt something tickling my toes I looked down," I explained. "At the time, I was holding the opened paint tin. When I saw the mouse I panicked, threw up my arms and ran."

At this point I wondered if I should have stuck with the 'loose plank' story. I could abandon the house, live rough, wander the streets clutching the paint pot and talking to myself. I dragged my mind back from my life as a bag lady to listen to Mike.

"Will I check out your kitchen for any wayward mice?" he repeated, louder.

"Yes." I breathed. That was an even better idea. "My hero," I murmured, as he strode bravely down the garden path.

"Did Mike say he's looking for mice?" Calum was back, sooner than expected, loaded down with every sort of hammer and nail in his father's toolbox.

"Yes," then, thinking quickly, "I spotted one slipping in the back door."

"Wow!" Calum climbed up beside me again. "You must have brilliant eyes!" he peered towards the door. "No wonder you know everything that happens in the classroom."

Yup, I was still holding my place on that pedestal.

Mike appeared in the doorway. "All clear!" he called.

I made my way gingerly down the path, but hesitated before peering through the open door. "How do you know it's not hiding behind the cooker, or something?"

Mike grinned. "Well, I could say it's due to the amazing tracking skills I've inherited from my American Indian ancestors." He crouched down, studying the ground. "Ah, yes, a hedgehog trampled over this blade of grass at precisely 3.38 this morning." He looked up. "But I think even you will see the mouse-shaped Arabian Sunset footprints disappearing under the Azaleas."

I grinned back. "I've gone off that colour, now." The thought of a mouse-free house was making me more confident. I twirled the paint pot, slowly. "Perhaps you could help me pick a better shade?"

Calum had been ignored for too long. "Mike's good with wood, and fires, and mice, and paint." He paused, then tugged on my paint splattered shirt to whisper confidentially, "but we'd better check for spiders, first. His mum always has to get rid of them."

"You mean the wonderful big cousin, firefighter Mike, is scared of spiders?" I laughed, staring at Mike.

Mike looked shamefaced. "OK, you deal with the spiders and I'll deal with the mice. And you," he ruffled Calum's hair, "keep your mouth shut from now on."

"Yes," I grinned, "after today, I'm sure we can cope with anything – even seven-year-olds!"

The Rock
by Fiona McFadzean

My surroundings fall away
Only the shape of the rock
towering in front of me
catches my eye and my breath.
I'm back in Gibraltar
snapping the apes, delighting
in their antics, laughing aloud
like I did in long ago summers.

Summers of golden sun and a
summer of silver jubilation
in honour of Her Majesty.
Excited children in fancy dress,
the priest clutching sausages,
a present brought from home.
The warmth of memory goes
leaving the chill of where I am.

For this is a different rock,
its evergreen skirt and snow
spattered top tell me so.
No Barbary residents here,
no camera happy tourists.
No mirth, no joy, naught
but a sullen silence and
the unshed tears of winter.

Only the glimmering hope
of Heaven's promised spring
keeping the Soul alive.

Getting Plastered
by Catherine Lang

Take a break, my friends all said,
enjoy the summer sun.
Now that you're retiring,
allow yourself some fun.

A trip I planned, a merry jaunt
to visit gay Paree.
A trip I took, a flying start;
I went to A&E.

Grim faced I sat, with gritted teeth
as plaster they applied.
A damaged wrist, a nasty break.
That could not be denied!

Just next to me, a little girl,
her cast a pinkish hue,
looked over at me earnestly.
"Whatever did you do?"

Falling over in the street –
it sounded very weak.
My mind was on the days ahead;
my summer looking bleak.

"I fell," I said quite briefly,
feeling less that proud.
The next few words from out her mouth
made me laugh out loud.

Amazing how an eight-year-old
can stop you feeling blue.
Her question, very simply,
"Were you turning cartwheels too?"

Cutting Loose
by Helena Sheridan

Jillian took a deep breath then blurted out her decision.

"I'm sorry, Michael, but it's over. I need to move on."

There. She'd said it. Even if the words were directed to the back of his head as he rummaged through the linen cupboard, now he knew – and no amount of pleading or pained sighs would change her mind this time.

Surprisingly, he didn't turn round and beg her to reconsider, but continued to finger through the stack of fresh towels, while tunelessly whistling a Sixties hit that came from the radio.

To think she'd spent sleepless nights choosing the right words, the right moment, then to be ignored!

There was only one thing to do. Jillian yanked the plug free from the wall, plunging them into silence.

"Did you hear me, Michael? I said…"

"I know what you said, it's the old 'I'm going to leave you' speech again, isn't it?" he said. "Give it a rest, why don't you, Jilly? It's been a long day."

Well, enough was enough. Perhaps if she started to pack he would take her seriously.

Storming into the back room, she rummaged for her holdall among the clutter of things collected in their eight months together. Each symbolised happier times. How different he had been in the beginning...

"Come on, love, let's give it a go. I know we can make it." Like a fool she had given in.

Jillian sighed. That had been her problem – she always gave in. It was like a well-rehearsed routine. Michael bullied, she fumed, and then, when she got really upset he applied the antidote – a liberal measure of syrupy compliments. But things were different now. Her future lay with Alan.

From the minute Alan moved into the street, she knew there would be trouble. Smart, good looking, with all the trappings of success, Alan seemed to have it all – but he wanted her too!

She recalled their first meeting. She'd been hurrying back from the supermarket with a pint of milk, when Alan came rushing around the corner and slammed into her. He quickly dispelled her embarrassment with a winning smile and that well-worn quip about 'spilt milk'. When he invited her for a compensatory coffee, she politely refused – as she did the second and third time they 'accidentally' met.

"Got you on a tight leash, has he?" Alan had joked.

Michael was anything but the perfect partner, but Alan was out of order, and she told him, albeit half-heartedly.

It wasn't until weeks later that things came to a head. Having spent the morning listening to Michael blame her for everything, she retreated to the local coffee shop, hoping to find Alan in his usual spot by the window.

His warm humour was just what she needed.

"Face it, Jilly, you're too good for him. Why not just end it? Can't you see he's using you? You know you'd be happier with me!"

Alan was right – she realised that now. The only answer was to cut and run...

Lifting the bulging holdall she glanced back into the other room. Michael was sitting with his feet on his desk, reading a magazine. Marching into the room, she knocked his legs off their perch.

"I meant what I said Michael," she tossed her head in defiance, "I've been seeing Alan Randall and...I want to be with him."

Michael slammed his hand on the desk. There was something worrying about the glint in his eyes.

"So that's it? It's over? Just like that!" He rounded the desk to confront her. "You're willing to toss all this away, because Alan Randall says he needs you? What about me? I need you."

Was the desperation in his voice just another act? Michael was capable of anything if he thought he'd lose out to his rival.

"I won't let him break us up!" he yelled, snatching a pair of scissors from the desk. He stroked the blades.

"Give me those," she pleaded, but he pushed her hand away.

With an exasperated sigh, Jillian lunged forward to wrench the scissors free, causing a frenzy of fingers, glimmering steel and blood...

He slumped into the chair to nurse a lacerated thumb.

"You can't keep them, they're mine!" Jillian snapped. "So are the combs, straighteners and that drier. I'll be back for them."

She stormed out of the salon. Working with Michael had been hair-raising. Hopefully her new job with Alan Randall Creations would be less so!

The Full Works
by Greta Yorke

I sit nervously waiting. I have never done this before. My husband was so attentive especially in those early days. My every whim in this department was totally and completely satisfied, but lately he had become less accommodating, disinterested even. That's why I'm here waiting for my pampering and, how exciting, being tempted by all those tantalising treatments. And you know what? I reckon I'm worth the full works!

Then he appears, my young eastern cleansing practitioner, treacle eyes smouldering, dark and somewhat sultry. He smiles warmly and I melt. I'm in his hands now and, oh, how good it feels.

I relax and prepare myself, as water gently trickles over me. Oh, I've waited so long for this. He stretches over me now as he drizzles me in rich foam. Now he tenderly massages in circular motion, producing a sumptuous lather which oozes through his flexed fingers. He is so close, so intimate, his skin so tanned but I find I'm not the least shy or embarrassed as he rinses me. Oh, if they could see me now, my friends, my husband.

Just when I'm thinking things can't get much better, another equally toned and muscular young man appears and they repeat my treatment of creamy whipped indulgence. This is so good.

I sense it will soon be all over and I want it prolonged as long as possible. I feel so cleansed all over, so fresh, so rejuvenated.

I'll not be back at the automatic car wash.

A Bit of Peace & Quiet
by Maggie Bolton

"I hope you won't find it too dull and quiet here after your busy life in London," said Mrs McDonald, as her new tenant plonked a huge box of groceries on the draining board. There was just the slightest trace of awe, or perhaps slight disapproval in the way she referred to 'London'. Her experience of cities was limited to the occasional trip to Glasgow and her impressions of London were gleaned only from the TV.

"I don't know that I'd like it myself; all that noise and traffic...and Beefeaters marching about," she added inexplicably.

"Pardon?" said Karen, "Oh, right. Yes. Well, I don't actually live in central London, more in the suburbs you know, so it's not so bad."

"Oh aye, the suburbs," said Mrs McDonald, nodding sagely.

"Actually, peace and quiet is just what I'm after," said Karen, "and the cottage is gorgeous!"

"Hmmm, well I hope you'll be comfortable. It's normally only a summer let, you understand, but it's a good, sound, wee house and there's plenty of cut peat at the back for your fire when the weather turns."

"Peat fires, goodness, how exciting! It was just gas heating in my flat."

Karen was aware that she was babbling, but she was actually a little un-nerved by the way Mrs McDonald was looking at her – rather as a member of a bomb-squad might regard a suspicious package.

"Is that a fact now?" said Mrs McDonald, "Well, if you're needing anything, you can always get me with the telephone and Archie or myself will come over. The number's on the pad."

"Thank you, you're very kind," said Karen.

At this point, rather to Karen's surprise, Mrs McDonald whipped out a fairly 'state-of-the-art' mobile phone from a pocket in her old-fashioned pinny.

"Mind you," she said, "sometimes the reception's no very good."

She held the phone a little distance away and squinted myopically at it as she stabbed at the keys, grunting with the concentration.

"ARCHIE!" she suddenly yelled at the inoffensive little device, "YOU CAN COME AND FETCH ME NOW. I'M WITH THE ENGLISH WOMAN…..WHAT?.....I CAN'T HEAR YOU…..WHAT?.....HUH!!!"

She stuck the phone ferociously back into her pinny.

"There now, is that no just like a man," she commented with disgust, "under your feet when you don't want them and never there when you do. He says he might be a while yet as Dougal has just poured him a dram and it wouldn't be polite to just toss it back and leave, now would it? That'll be him for the next hour I dare say."

"Oh well, perhaps I could give you a lift," Karen offered.

Mrs McDonald gave her a pitying, disbelieving look. "How?" she asked, "Ye havenae got a boat!"

"*Boat*?" said Karen, "Oh! Oh yes I see now. When you said if I phoned you'd come over, you meant you'd come...*over*, as in 'across the loch'. I just thought you meant you'd...er...come over." I'm babbling again, she thought.

Mrs McDonald said nothing but her face spoke volumes.

"Well, in the meantime, would you like a cup of tea or something, or perhaps you'd prefer 'a wee dram' yourself?" suggested Karen rather self-consciously.

She retrieved a packet of tea-bags and a small bottle of whisky from the box of groceries and held them up enquiringly.

"Well, I'm sure that's very civil of you, Miss Evans," said Mrs McDonald, "I'll take a cup of tea with you then."

"Oh, call me Karen," she said, taking her new, cordless kettle out of another box.

"Now isn't that a coincidence," said Mrs McDonald, "I've just bought the very same kettle as that myself. I got it with the mail order, you know."

She placed equal and significant emphasis on the words 'mail' and 'order', as if she didn't want Karen to confuse it with the '*fe*-mail order', which might also be available.

"Really?" said Karen, "Is that where you got your mobile too? It looks pretty new."

"Aye, pokey wee thing that it is," said Mrs McDonald scathingly, "I used to have a bigger one. It was *much* better, but it was no use for the text-messages you see?"

"Is that a fact?" said Karen, unwittingly copying Mrs McDonald's turn of phrase. She handed over a steaming cup of tea and they sipped companionably.

"So, you're a teacher then?" said Mrs McDonald.

"Mmmm," said Karen without enthusiasm, "but I haven't been too well lately; 'stress related' according to the doctor." She paused and stared gloomily into her tea-cup. "To be honest," she went on, "I don't think teaching is quite for me; I'm not particularly good at it I'm afraid. I'd rather be a writer. The doctor said maybe a sabbatical would be a good idea, so I could try my hand at writing for a while. So, that's why I came up here."

Mrs McDonald looked, by turns, interested, sympathetic, puzzled, and then a little worried.

"Oh dear," she said, "I'm no very sure you'd be able to get one of those *sub-articles* hereabouts, even with the mail order."

Karen smothered a giggle and decided a quick change of subject was required. She stood up and went to the door.

"Wow! This view is just stunning!" she said.

The water of the loch glinted in the sunlight. On the far side, successive lines of hills became bluer and bluer into the distance. Her little white-washed cottage sat, with its identical neighbour, under the lee of a towering mountainside. The mountain dwarfed them, making them no more significant than the sheep, which showed up only as white dots in the blue and green landscape. Mrs McDonald joined her and surveyed the scene with obvious pride.

"Aye," she said, "I don't know that you could ever find a better view than that."

"Is there anyone in the other cottage?" Karen asked.

"Oh yes," said Mrs McDonald. Then she chuckled. "I'm getting very posh; I've a writer in one of my cottages, and an artist in the other! He's only there until the end of August of course – Sandy Corrigan his name is. He makes wood-carvings. Very striking they are, and they sell very well, so he tells me. I don't know that they're quite my cup of tea though."

Karen wondered if they were nude figures or very abstract with lots of holes in or something. She would investigate later.

Suddenly, out of nowhere, came an ear-blasting, chest-vibrating roar that built to a crescendo and then died away as quickly as it came.

"J-e-e-es! What was *that*?" asked Karen in alarm.

Mrs McDonald seemed unconcerned.

"That? Oh, it's just the RAF," she said, "a Tornado I think. Of course, they're not supposed to fly low over the village, but maybe they think that just one or two wee houses by the loch-side don't count."

"Good grief! Do they do that often?" asked Karen, recovering from the shock.

"Hmmm, well, now and again maybe," said Mrs McDonald evasively. "Oh look, here comes Archie."

The following morning Karen woke early. The water of the loch was dark and clear and absolutely still and the air had a clarity and calmness that she had rarely experienced before. With a sigh of satisfaction, she sat down to eat her breakfast beside the water. She would go for a short walk and then at 9 o'clock she would begin to write. She had decided to be severe with herself and work a set number of hours each day, or nothing would get done. As she passed her neighbour's cottage she saw, in a lean-to, what was obviously 'work-in-progress'. A huge chunk of timber, a tree-trunk in fact, had been secured, upright, to a broader base. Though unfinished, the expressive attitude of the human figure was, as Mrs McDonald had said, striking. Something about the rough-hewn quality of the wood, which still had sections of bark in places, gave the work a wonderful vitality.

"Like it?" said a voice.

"It's terrific," said Karen. "Hi, you must be Sandy Corrigan. I'm Karen Evans."

"I know," said Sandy.

"That is beautiful – so raw and alive!" said Karen enthusiastically. "How do you get it to look like that?"

"Like this," he said. He was obviously a man of few words.

Donning safety goggles, he pulled the starter on a huge chain-saw, which Karen had somehow failed to notice. With a few controlled sweeps, he fashioned the flowing folds of a dress and the elegant turn of the figure's head.

"I do the detail with a hammer and chisel later," yelled Sandy over the rasping whine of the saw.

"Terrific," said Karen again rather weakly, with her hands over her ears.

9o'clock

Sitting at the table, staring at a blank computer screen, Karen waited for inspiration to strike. It took its time. Eventually though, she began and soon became engrossed in the world of her creative imagination. The chain-saw's intermittent whine wasn't *too* distracting. She persevered. A distant humming grew suddenly louder. Ah, but she was ready for them this time. The Tornados had lost their power to alarm – pretty annoying though. Then the phone rang. I knew the phone was a bad idea, she thought.

"Hello?....Oh hello mum…..yes, got here just fine; no trouble at all…..Oh just beautiful! It's right on the edge of a loch – fantastic views…..Yes…..Yes, she seems very nice. She said if I need anything, to ring and she'll come over…..over from the other side of the loch, she means, ha ha!....What?...."

Another Tornado blasted through the calm. Sandy took another swing at his masterpiece.

"What?....Do I *want* anything?....Well, a bit of peace and quiet might be nice."

The LiterEight Writers

Fiona Atchison has had poetry published in various magazines and won the Scottish Association of Writers (SAW) poetry competition in 2005. A winning crime story was printed in an anthology, *Ayr 800* and performed in front of an audience, and in 2010 she entered the SAW crime novel competition and gained third place. She won the SAW inaugural science fiction competition in 2008 sponsored by *Writers' News* and was published on their website. A surprise win of a song lyric competition led to collaboration with a singer/songwriter and produced three CDs. In 2011 a couple of her children's picture book stories were published by *Ice Water Press*.

Maggie Bolton is English by birth but has lived in Scotland with her husband for the past twenty odd years (not all *that* odd). She taught both in the UK and in Germany and now retains contact with children as a Rainbow Guide Leader. No surprise then that her main interest is children's writing, but also enjoys other writing forms, provided it's not too serious (Don't look for 'deep and meaningful' unless you have a lot of time to waste.) She is also a painter, exhibiting locally and would like to break into illustration.

Helena Sheridan was born in Biggleswade. Her family emigrated to Melbourne, Australia, returning to the UK in 1976 and she now lives in Scotland. Her keen interest in drama has resulted in her plays and comedy monologues being performed in various Scottish theatres. She has also written children's educational scripts for BBC Radio Ulster and is published in women's fiction, poetry and articles both in the UK and abroad. She would dearly love to write more if only she could stop playing Mahjong!

Lesley Deschner enjoys writing short stories, articles, humorous poems, sketches and plays. Her passion for acting has introduced her to local Ayrshire theatre companies, such as Hipshot and Polymorph with whom she has taken roles. Lesley is a Council Member of the Scottish Association of Writers and is Secretary Assistant to the Writers' Summer School in Swanwick, Derbyshire. She is planning to raid her ideas file for new stories, finish her 'works in progress' and submit them for publication.

Janice Johnston has lived on the same Ayrshire farm for most of her life. She has written for a good chunk of that time, too, but only seriously from the mid-90s. She joined a local writers' club and began to have success with children's short stories and woman's magazine short stories. She has been published in magazines in Australia and South Africa, as well as the UK. For a number of years, she wrote scripts for education programmes for BBC radio. When not writing, she helps her husband on the farm and tries to keep track of her two (almost) grown up sons.

Catherine Lang started writing in her teens and her love of words led to a life-long career in public affairs. She wrote on myriad topics – briefing materials, speeches, feature articles – and her work regularly appeared in print and electronic media. For the past decade she has added fiction, poetry and drama to her portfolio and has enjoyed success both in competition and in publication.

Fiona McFadzean was hooked on writing after winning a National Competition in primary school, enjoying drama and poetry in particular. For many years she wrote sketches, revues and plays for amateur dramatics and youth theatre. She has also devised training programmes for Adult Literacy and modified GCSE coursework for students with Special Educational Needs while working in Education. She has also taught creative writing to adults and teenagers. After serving on various writing committees, Fiona decided that it was time to concentrate on her personal output and, at present, is working on both a crime and a romantic novel.

Greta Yorke is a retired primary teacher who lives in west Scotland. Story writing started at school where she transformed jotters into storybooks, but she did not begin writing seriously until 2008 when she joined Ayr Writers' Club. Since then she has enjoyed success when her children's story won first place in the Scottish Association of Writers' Competition in 2010. She has had poetry and articles published, in addition to children's stories online.

www.litereight.co.uk

Notes

Coming Soon

Look out for LiterEight's next collection, *Dark Twists*.

Printed in Poland
by Amazon Fulfillment
Poland Sp. z o.o., Wrocław